She caught him watching her.

Hailey welcomed his presence. His strength. His support.

She slid a glance at the one-time bad boy, caught his profile, the square cut of his chin, the angular cheekbones. Something told her there was still a bit of rebel in the detective, something she found far more appealing than she should.

Don't get too close, her conscience ordered. Nick Granger may be easy to lean on today, but he's not the kind of man you want or need.

And he wasn't.

Even if he did happen to be her temporary lover.

And the father of her baby.

Dear Reader,

Well, we hope your New Year's resolutions included reading some fabulous new books—because we can provide the reading material! We begin with *Stranded with the Groom* by Christine Rimmer, part of our new MONTANA MAVERICKS: GOLD RUSH GROOMS miniseries. When a staged wedding reenactment turns into the real thing, can the actual honeymoon be far behind? Tune in next month for the next installment in this exciting new continuity.

Victoria Pade concludes her NORTHBRIDGE NUPTIALS miniseries with *Having the Bachelor's Baby,* in which a woman trying to push aside memories of her one night of passion with the town's former bad boy finds herself left with one little reminder of that encounter—she's pregnant with his child. Judy Duarte begins her new miniseries, BAYSIDE BACHELORS, with *Hailey's Hero,* featuring a cautious woman who finds herself losing her heart to a rugged rebel who might break it…. THE HATHAWAYS OF MORGAN CREEK by Patricia Kay continues with *His Best Friend,* in which a woman is torn between two men—the one she really wants, and the one to whom he owes his life. Mary J. Forbes's sophomore Special Edition is *A Father, Again,* featuring a grown-up reunion between a single mother and her teenaged crush. And a disabled child, an exhausted mother and a down-but-not-out rodeo hero all come together in a big way, in Christine Wenger's debut novel, *The Cowboy Way.*

So enjoy, and come back next month for six compelling new novels, from Silhouette Special Edition.

Happy New Year!

Gail Chasan
Senior Editor
Silhouette Special Edition

Please address questions and book requests to:
Silhouette Reader Service
U.S.: 3010 Walden Ave., P.O. Box 1325, Buffalo, NY 14269
Canadian: P.O. Box 609, Fort Erie, Ont. L2A 5X3

Hailey's Hero

JUDY DUARTE

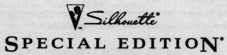

SPECIAL EDITION®

Published by Silhouette Books

America's Publisher of Contemporary Romance

To Christy Freetly and Gail Duarte, who spent hours reading my books
in manuscript form, even those drafts that may never see the light of day.
If God hadn't made us family, I would have chosen you both as friends.

And to Mahnita Boyden-Wofford, who turned a blind eye when I
played hooky from the day job to dream up stories and chat with
my critique partners on the telephone. Thanks for looking
out for our family over the years.

 SILHOUETTE BOOKS

ISBN 0-373-24659-5

HAILEY'S HERO

Copyright © 2005 by Judy Duarte

Visit Silhouette Books at www.eHarlequin.com

Printed in U.S.A.

Books by Judy Duarte

Silhouette Special Edition

Cowboy Courage #1458
Family Practice #1511
Almost Perfect #1540
Big Sky Baby #1563
The Virgin's Makeover #1593
Bluegrass Baby #1598
The Rich Man's Son #1634
Hailey's Hero #1659

Silhouette Books

Double Destiny
"Second Chance"

JUDY DUARTE

An avid reader who enjoys a happy ending, Judy Duarte always wanted to write books of her own. One day, she decided to make that dream come true. Five years and six manuscripts later, she sold her first book to Silhouette Special Edition.

Her unpublished stories have won the Emily and the Orange Rose, and in 2001, she became a double Golden Heart finalist. Judy credits her success to Romance Writers of America and two wonderful critique partners, Sheri WhiteFeather and Crystal Green, both of whom write for Silhouette.

At times, when a stubborn hero and a headstrong heroine claim her undivided attention, she and her family are thankful for fast food, pizza delivery and video games. When she's not at the keyboard or in a Walter Mitty–type world, she enjoys traveling, spending romantic evenings with her personal hero and playing board games with her kids.

Judy lives in Southern California and loves to hear from her readers. You may write to her at: P.O. Box 498, San Luis Rey, CA 92068-0498. You can also visit her Web site at www.judyduarte.com.

Dear Reader,

Welcome to Bayside, a fictitious beachfront community near sunny San Diego, where love and romance await the unsuspecting men known as the Bayside Bachelors.

This new miniseries has one common thread. All of the heroes were once troubled teens—bad boys—who turned their lives around thanks to the guidance of Harry Logan, a retired detective who took them under his wing.

In each book, you'll meet everyday heroes like cops and firemen, doctors and navy pilots, men who can't quite shake a stubborn heart, a crooked smile or the rebellious nature that still flows in their veins. I don't know about you, but I've always liked stories of redemption, stories of regular people who overcame the odds and made tremendous and, oftentimes, heroic changes in their lives.

I had fun creating the Bayside Bachelors and the women who would touch their hearts. May you experience that same pleasure as you turn each page, as you enter the world of Harry and Kay Logan, meet the men they've grown to care about and watch each romance unfold.

Wishing you all the best,

Judy Duarte

Chapter One

Hailey Conway didn't believe in heroes. And hadn't since her sixth birthday.

Over the years, she'd accepted the fact that a woman couldn't expect someone to rescue her, to step in and make life picture-book perfect.

So when Hailey walked out of the Granville drugstore and a young man jerked on her black vinyl purse, she didn't scream for help. Instead, she struggled with the thug until he knocked her fanny-first on the sidewalk.

At the gas station across the street, a tall, dark-haired stranger in a leather jacket yelled to the attendant to call the police, then took off in pursuit of Hailey's mugger.

Heart pounding and hands trembling, she stood on

wobbly legs and grimaced at the pain in her right hip. She didn't think anything was broken, but her bottom hurt like the dickens. She brushed the dirt from her wool slacks and looked down the street. Both suspect and stranger were long gone.

And so was her oversize purse. But it wasn't her cash and credit cards she worried about. It was the package she'd discreetly slipped inside that concerned her. A package she'd traveled twenty miles to buy.

Now she was not only missing her purse and her purchase, she was rubbing an aching rear end.

A police cruiser pulled to a stop in front of the drugstore, and a stocky, red-haired officer climbed from the car. "What seems to be the problem, ma'am?"

Hailey explained what had happened, then pointed in the direction the mugger and the stranger had run.

"Your name?" he asked.

"Hailey Conway." She hoped she wouldn't have to list the contents of her missing purse. Wallet, thirty-seven dollars in cash, a library card, house keys, a pack of spearmint gum.

And a brand-new box of condoms.

Sheesh. She'd never purchased prophylactics before, had never needed to. But she had big plans for the evening, big enough to make her brave a pending winter storm and travel to a nearby town where she desperately hoped the Walden School librarian wouldn't be recognized.

So far, her identity was safe, but the whole experience had been a nightmare of embarrassment. The elderly cashier had fumbled about, looking for a small bag, while the darn condoms lay in plain sight on the countertop. Hailey had told the slow-moving woman not to bother and quickly stashed the box and receipt in her purse.

"Is that the guy, ma'am?" The burly policeman nodded up the sidewalk, where the stranger had brought the mugger to justice.

If Hailey wasn't mistaken, it appeared the teenage hoodlum wore handcuffs. "Yes. The big kid in the blue ski jacket is the one who stole my purse and knocked me down."

The officer took her address for his report. "Wait here," he told her before proceeding down the street toward the apprehended mugger. The dark-haired stranger withdrew his ID, a badge of some kind, which seemed to satisfy the Granville patrolman.

While the thief was read his rights, then placed into the police car, the stranger sauntered toward Hailey carrying her purse. He had the look of a guy who wasn't afraid to take chances, of one who'd seen the seedy side of life. A man who didn't belong in what was supposed to be a crime-free small town. A worn, black leather aviator jacket suggested he didn't even belong in Minnesota during the winter.

Dark-brown eyes, the color of fresh-perked coffee, pierced her soul, stimulating her pulse.

"Are you all right?" he asked, his voice deep and slightly graveled.

"Fine," she said, although her bottom still hurt.

He handed her the purse, and she clutched it to her chest like a shield, protecting her from his caffeine-laden gaze and the quirk of a smile that taunted her senses without betraying his thoughts.

"Thank you."

"No problem." He stood tall, more than six feet. Not handsome in the classic sense, but attractive in a young Marlon Brando way.

If she were the kind of woman in search of a hero, this guy would fit the bill. But she wasn't looking for a savior. In her experience the heroic side of a man only masked flaws of one kind or another. Heroes were just regular guys who sometimes did something honorable.

And sometimes didn't.

He nodded toward her black vinyl shield. "You'd better check and make sure everything is there."

Open her purse? With the telltale box of condoms shoved on top? Bare her secrets in front of this stranger? "I'm sure everything is fine. Thank you for going after that guy and getting my purse back."

"No problem," he said, as though he risked his life and chased danger on a daily basis.

She offered him a smile, yet held tightly to the ugly but serviceable handbag, her palms sweating in spite of the chill in the air. Surely he'd forget about asking her to peek inside.

"Better take a look," he said, tapping the bag with his finger.

Hailey stepped back and, in an effort to pull the vinyl bag from his reach, the darn purse slipped from her hands and dropped to the ground. In a frozen stupor, she watched the shiny new box of condoms slide onto the sidewalk, all the while praying a hole in the concrete would swallow her up. But she remained standing, her gaze locked on his.

A slow grin tugged on his lips. "Shoplifting?"

"Absolutely not." Hailey stooped and shoved the box back in her purse. "I have a receipt. You can ask the cashier."

"I'll take your word for it."

When she stood, he flashed her a sexy, Marlon Brando smile. She didn't return it. "Like I said, I have everything I need."

The moment the statement left her mouth, heat flooded her cheeks. She'd implied that she needed condoms. Darn that man for flustering her so.

"The name's Nick Granger. I'm an off-duty detective." He flashed her a badge of some kind, but she didn't take the time to look at it closely, particularly since it had passed the police officer's scrutiny.

Ever since her sixth birthday, Hailey had sworn off cops, particularly handsome detectives. As far as she was concerned, they were never around when you needed them.

Of course, this particular cop had been.

"Thanks for your help," she said. "Now if you'll excuse me, I have to go home and fix dinner."

Nick bit back a laugh. He didn't usually tease a crime victim, but the rosy-cheeked brunette who hid condoms in her purse had touched his funny bone, not to mention his libido.

The petite young woman had a pretty face, with long chestnut hair and eyes the color of a summer sky. But it was more than her looks that he found arousing. It was the way she lifted her chin and showed a stubborn sense of pride. The flash of spunk, as she pulled herself together. The shy, awkward way she wanted to hide the condoms from him.

He watched her limp away and climb into a ten-year-old Honda Accord. Some guy was going to get lucky tonight, and he couldn't help wondering who it would be.

A husband?

No, not a spouse. She was too flustered about the condoms, too shy about them for that. A secret lover then? The idea warmed Nick's blood and made him grin. He wouldn't mind being the lover in question.

Whoa. Back up. He hadn't come to Minnesota to fantasize about an affair with a stranger. He had a mission.

He was looking for a woman who lived in Walden, a small farm town about twenty miles from here. The attendant at the gas station had been explaining how he could reach the county road that would take him there when Nick had spotted the purse-snatching in action.

A cold wind blew out of the north, hinting at the snow to come. Nick zipped his black leather jacket. Minnesota was a hell of a lot colder than southern California.

When he left home this morning, the weatherman had predicted a sunny day in the high eighties. And had his old friend and mentor not needed his services, Nick would have spent the afternoon on the sands of Pacific Beach.

But late last night, Harry Logan had called from his hospital bed to ask a favor, and Nick hadn't given the request a second thought. He owed the retired detective—big-time. If not for Harry's involvement in Nick's sorry life, he might be rotting in prison right now. Or dead.

Harry had given more than one angry delinquent reason to look beyond a crappy childhood. And Nick had found himself wanting to be a man of honor, a man like Harry. It was a goal Nick would never reach, though, because the old man had raised the bar too damn high.

His loyalty ran deep for the aging detective, and like each one of the other twelve or thirteen guys known as Logan's Heroes, Nick would do anything for Harry. Nick owed the man far more than a trip to Minnesota on the cusp of winter. A hell of a lot more.

Harry had taken Nick to ball games and invited him to backyard barbecues. He'd even paid Nick's first semester registration at the local junior college, making him feel as much a part of the Logan family as Harry's own sons.

"Hailey's my daughter," Harry had said. "And she's living in a small Minnesota farm town. I want you to bring her to San Diego. To the hospital, where I can see her. Where I can talk to her. I let her down a long time ago, and I want to apologize, ask her forgiveness.''

Nick found it hard to believe Harry could have let anyone down. Ever. He was too much of a straight-arrow. Too dedicated to his family and the youth in the community. Youth at risk, as Nick had been.

Nick had plenty of questions, but he wasn't about to force his old friend to say more than he wanted to.

''Find Hailey Conway,'' Harry had asked Nick from his hospital bed.

It was as simple as that.

Nick looked at his watch. The sooner he found the woman, the better. He'd promised Harry not to return to San Diego without her.

It was a promise Nick intended to keep.

Hailey pulled aside the lace curtain and looked out the living room window. The sky had darkened to a threatening gray, giving credibility to the weatherman who'd announced a winter storm warning and predicted the next snow would be fierce and unusually cold.

The first flakes began to sprinkle the ground, laying claim to the dormant grass that hid below the frozen surface. The temperature had dropped considerably since she'd left Granville well over an hour ago.

Had Steven made it out of Mankato before the worst of the blustery storm hit? Hailey hoped he didn't get stranded along the way, because she had big plans for tonight. And condoms in the nightstand to prove it.

She thought about the episode in town, about the good-looking detective who'd known what she had planned for the evening, but quickly shoved the awkward memory aside. She'd had her first and last bittersweet run-in with a cop when she was six years old. A man she'd looked up to, until he abandoned her mother.

Nope. Harry Logan hadn't deserved the hero worship a starry-eyed child had offered him. That's why she'd refused to talk to him when he'd called her after twenty years. A personal relationship with the man who'd fathered her was the last thing in the world she wanted.

Since moving to Minnesota, Hailey had set her sights on home, hearth and a man she could trust. And she'd fought too long and hard for her goals to become distracted now.

The little house she'd purchased with her own earnings had grown warm and cozy, and the aroma of roast beef filled the air. She glanced over her shoulder at the table she'd set for two and smiled at the result of her careful preparation. China, crystal wineglasses, tapered candlesticks.

She'd invited Steven to dinner again. The hard-working accountant lived alone and made no bones about how much he enjoyed a home-cooked meal.

The way to a man's heart was through his stomach, the old adage said. And just in case a hearty meal of meat and potatoes wasn't enough to make

Steven pop the question, or at least make a commitment, Hailey had an alternate route to his heart—a
well-plotted but subtle seduction.

It had been a long time since she'd been intimate
with a man, too long, probably. In college she'd
found herself attracted to the wrong kind of guy, the
kind who promised sexual fulfillment but couldn't
offer anything long-term. When she realized her pen-
chant for falling for the devil-may-care type, she'd
made it a point to look for the right kind of mate,
even if he didn't sweep her off her feet.

She'd worked hard to make her world predictable
and stable. And she intended to choose a husband in
the same way she'd selected the little house and the
dependable car she drove—with a great deal of care
and foresight.

Steven was her soon-to-be fiancé, although he
didn't know it yet. There weren't too many men like
the brilliant accountant. Handsome. Gentle. Honest.
Loyal. He was a good neighbor, as well as a friend.
His smile might not make her heart soar or do flip-
flops, but it did warm her soul. And she had no
qualms about pursuing a physical relationship with
him.

A glass or two of wine would take the edge off
her nervousness. Any more than that, and she just
might lose her head. Visions of Lois Lane removing
Clark Kent's glasses and kissing him senseless
crossed her mind, and she quickly pushed it aside.
This evening was more than a romantic game.

A knock sounded at the door, drawing her from

her daydreams. It was probably little Tommy Kuehn looking for his cat again or Mrs. Billings, the elderly woman who lived next door, wanting to share a cup of coffee. Those were the kinds of visitors Hailey had grown to expect in the small community in which she'd chosen to settle down and make a home.

She opened the door and bit back a gasp when she spotted the rugged detective on her stoop, the man who had apprehended the mugger and returned her purse. Her heart began to race.

He seemed nearly as surprised to see her as she was to see him, but he smiled, masking his thoughts, so it seemed.

What was he doing here? Had he taken her name from the police report? Was this official business? Would she need to go to court?

"Yes?" She leaned against the door, blocking him from entering the house, from getting too close, and scanned his broad length. Her gaze focused on a snow-speckled head of unruly dark hair that curled at the collar, a strong, aquiline nose that had probably been broken a time or two, a small but jagged scar that marred the left brow.

"Hailey Conway?"

She merely nodded, not trusting her own voice.

"I had a tough time finding your place."

She didn't doubt it. Some of the graveled streets didn't have signs. "I guess you're not from around here."

"I'm not."

That didn't surprise her. But she figured it might

be a good idea to take a look at the badge he'd flashed the police officer earlier. "Do you have some ID?"

He showed her his badge, and she looked it over this time.

A detective. From San Diego.

"You're a long way from home."

"Hopefully I can get back to the airport soon. Weather's a heck of a lot nicer where I come from."

His stance mimicked that of a private eye, the kind seen on television. The kind women tuned in to watch on a lonely Saturday night. She could imagine him as a star.

The Nielson ratings would probably skyrocket for his show, particularly with the female fans. He had a fearsomely attractive way about him, as though he'd just stepped off the set of *On the Waterfront* and "could'a been a contender."

"I came to check on you," he said. "See if you're all right after that tumble you took."

He was going above and beyond the call of hero duty, and Hailey hoped he'd leave before Steven arrived. She had half a notion to close the door in his face, but the guy had gone out of his way to chase down her mugger. She owed him some courtesy, to say the least. "I'm fine. Thanks."

"Can I come in? It's cold out here, and I'd like to talk to you."

No, she wanted to say. But she figured he'd come to ask her something about the purse snatching. She loosened her hold on the door and stepped aside.

Nick entered the warmth of Hailey Conway's house, and even though he wanted to cut to the chase and tell her why he was here, why he'd come all the way from California on a moment's notice looking for her, he held his tongue.

He hadn't expected her to be easy to convince. After Harry had tracked her down, found her phone number and gathered the courage to call, she'd given him what Harry referred to as ''a well-deserved'' piece of her mind and then promptly hung up.

Nick had expected Hailey to be older, especially since Harry and Kay had been married for forty years and had three sons, one of whom had been killed during Desert Storm.

Her age—mid-twenties—had surprised him, since he'd assumed she'd been the child of a previous marriage. But she'd obviously been conceived during the Logans' marriage. That surprised him, too, but it wasn't Nick's place to judge Harry about an affair.

''I lost touch with her twenty years ago,'' Harry had said. ''And I'm not sure I can fix things now, but I've got to try. I've got a lot of explaining to do, and not much time to do it.''

Nick slid the small brunette an assessing glance. As a detective, he'd learned to read people, their body language, their surroundings. He'd learned to keep a poker face, to hide his emotions and his assumptions. But recognizing the petite, dark-haired beauty with the bluest eyes he'd ever seen had knocked him for a loop.

Apparently, she was angry enough at Harry to

hang up the phone, rather than try to establish a relationship with the father she hadn't seen in years. Nick supposed there was more to the story than met the eye. But that didn't negate the promise he'd made to his friend and mentor.

Maybe Nick needed to play good cop for a while, before dropping Harry's name.

Still, he couldn't stifle his curiosity, and studied the pretty young woman who bore little resemblance to Harry.

She'd changed her clothes. Instead of winter wear, she had on a simple black dress. Not too revealing, but a hell of a nice fit.

"Have a seat," she said, indicating an overstuffed, floral-print sofa.

He sank into the cushions, his knees hitting a glass coffee table where a copy of *Better Homes and Gardens* rested next to an issue of *Modern Brides*. He glanced at her left hand, noting the absence of a ring, diamond or otherwise.

"Getting married?" he asked.

"No." A blush on her cheeks indicated embarrassment. She quickly broke eye contact, suggesting a lie or a reluctance to let him in on her private affairs. Still, the knowledge of those condoms lay before them in the awkward silence.

The aroma of pot roast filled the room. A small table in the dining room was set for two, along with wineglasses and new, red tapered candles. Nick slid her a slow smile. "No wedding bells, huh? Maybe the groom just doesn't know it yet."

She quickly stood, crossed her arms and flashed him a look of annoyance. The flush on her cheeks deepened, suggesting his comment had struck a chord of some kind. Then she scooped the magazines from the tabletop and placed them in a wicker basket that held other publications. "Did you have something to discuss with me?"

At this rate, Nick had better work on his manners and his ability to reason with her. Maybe he ought to turn on the charm, make nice, then hit her with his plan to take her to California. He'd leave Harry out of the discussion for the time being. "It looked as though you landed on the sidewalk kind of hard. Head injuries can be deceptive."

She crossed her arms under her breasts, drawing his attention to the way they would fill a man's hands.

Hell. Where had that misguided thought come from?

"My head is fine. And I bruised my…hip. Nothing's broken." The phone rang, interrupting the rest of her words. "Excuse me."

She turned and walked toward the kitchen. The hem of her black midlength dress brushed against shapely calves. She was a striking young woman, Nick realized. And stubborn. He wondered whether he could break down her defenses. Touch some tender spot in her heart and make her agree to see Harry.

Not if he didn't stop thinking about her as an attractive woman. A man didn't hit on his friend's daughter.

Nick scanned the small living room of the house she'd made into a home: floral-printed cotton, coordinating plaid pillows with ruffles, light oak furniture. Sheesh, Hailey was a nester—just the kind of woman Nick tried to avoid.

If there was one thing he didn't need, it was a woman who expected a guy to be home by five and spend weekends doing fix-it projects. Nick wasn't Ward Cleaver or Tim the Tool Man, nor did he want to be.

On the fireplace mantel, delicate picture frames— some silver, some crystal—displayed photographs. The feminine touch revealed a romantic side of the young woman, an emotional side he hoped to tap into.

He glanced to the kitchen, where she stood talking on the telephone. He figured she was going to ask him to leave. Well, what did he expect? A dinner invitation? His stomach grumbled like a small kid in the back seat clamoring for attention.

After talking to Harry at the hospital late last night, he'd gone home, packed his bags and headed for Lindbergh Field, hoping to catch an early-morning flight. He probably should have picked up a burger and fries along the way, but he'd been intent upon finding Hailey before checking into a hotel or grabbing a bite to eat. That might have been a mistake, he realized, as his stomach rumbled again. He should have eaten more at the airport than a sweet roll and black coffee, but he had been determined to reach Walden before the storm hit.

While Hailey talked quietly in the kitchen, Nick stood and made his way to the fireplace. He lifted a silver, heart-framed photograph from the mantel. A picture of a dark-haired girl in pigtails, missing a front tooth and straddling a two-wheeled bike, smiled at him, begging him to get to know the daughter Harry had let down.

He glanced at Hailey, who stood in a tidy, well-stocked kitchen. She had those cupboard doors that were mostly glass, the kind you could see right through. Every plate, cup and glass had been neatly stacked. Each can of vegetables lined carefully in a row. He thought of his own kitchen back home.

Thank goodness no one could see how he'd shoved his junk in each cupboard. And the drawers seemed to collect stuff he wasn't ready to throw away yet. It was a man's place, he noted. Just the way a guy liked it.

"Well, sure," Hailey told the person on the other line. "I understand. I'm disappointed, but I'll save you some leftovers."

The guy who was going to have a candlelit dinner of roast beef? Too bad. Fast food, Nick's usual dinner fare, wouldn't taste half as good as this meal smelled. He actually felt sorry for the guy. Sort of.

He looked at Hailey again, watched as she balanced the phone on one shoulder and checked the pot in the oven. She looked at home in a kitchen. Competent and capable. A real homebody, the kind

Nick steered clear of ever since that time he'd let Carla move into his apartment—a big mistake on his part.

Carla had questioned his every move and never understood why he couldn't leave a stakeout to be home by the time dinner was ready. Nope, a cop needed a different kind of woman. One that didn't expect promises a guy couldn't keep.

"When do they expect the storm to let up?" Hailey asked the caller.

So Hailey's dream date wasn't going to make it at all.

She twirled her finger around the phone cord, then glanced Nick's way. When their eyes met, something unspoken passed between them. An awareness, he supposed, of each other. The attraction he'd felt earlier and shoved aside muscled its way back—front and center. It caught him off guard. Her, too, he guessed, because she quickly turned her back to him.

"Take care, Steven. Bye." The telephone clicked against the wall mount as she hung up the receiver, and several moments of silence followed.

"Does Steven have a last name?" Nick didn't know why he asked.

"Not one that matters," she said. "If you have something to talk about, you'd better get it said. The storm has hit hard just south of here, and at least one road is closed."

He needed more time with her, time to figure out a good way to broach the subject and explain why he was here. And he needed time to understand why she wouldn't speak to Harry and how Nick could persuade her to change her mind.

When he didn't respond, she shook her head, then walked to the window and gazed out. She sighed heavily. "It's snowing. You'd better get out of here before it's too late to get back to your hotel. Where are you staying?"

"I haven't gotten a room yet. I wanted to check on you first."

"Didn't you hear the storm warning?"

"I hadn't planned on flying to Minnesota until late last night. I've got a change of clothes in a duffel bag in the car, along with a shaving kit. I'm not really prepared for a long, winter stay." Nick joined her at the window. He didn't get much chance to see snow, other than a couple of trips to the mountains near Julian.

"Well, you're in one heck of a fix, then. It's coming down hard and fast."

"Where's the nearest hotel?" he asked.

"South of here. Ten miles down the closed road."

"And the nearest hamburger joint?"

"Next door to the hotel." She leaned against the windowsill and crossed her arms, again lifting her breasts into mounds begging to be touched. "It looks like you've got a big problem."

Nick nodded, feeling a bit smug about the predicament that had forced Hailey's hand. She couldn't very well send him away now, could she?

Getting snowed in would definitely work in his favor, though. He would use the time to convince her to return to San Diego with him, to talk to Harry. He flashed her a smile that seemed to bounce off the rim without scoring a point.

She stepped closer, arms still crossed. The light, powdery scent of lilac accosted him with a frightening awareness of her femininity, of her proximity. He shook off the unwelcome temptation. Hailey Conway was off-limits, as far as he was concerned. But being stranded with her for a few hours might be the break he needed.

Her eyes sparkled, but not in pleasure. "I can't believe you'd drive all the way out here without checking the weather report, without having winter clothing. Don't you plan ahead?"

The only plan he'd had this morning was catching the first possible flight to Minneapolis. And he'd heard the damn weather report. But his goal had been finding her as quickly as possible, so he could take her back to California. Getting holed up in a motel wasn't part of his game plan.

Of course, getting stranded in a small house with a pretty but spunky brunette hadn't been part of the plan either, but he'd make it work. "I don't suppose I could pay you for a serving of roast beef? And maybe bunk out on your sofa?"

Those sky-blue eyes opened wide, as though he'd suggested they have a brief, meaningless love affair. The idea, he realized, was far more tempting than it should be.

Her arms dropped to her sides, and her lips parted. "Are you out of your mind?"

"Nope. Passed my psychological evaluations with flying colors. Or at least passable colors." He smiled, trying to lighten her mood.

It didn't work.

At least he hadn't told her his real reason for coming. Mentioning Harry right now would probably get him tossed out on his ear.

And it was too damn cold to risk that.

"It's either your sofa or my car," he said, hoping the pretty woman would have mercy on a well-meaning cop. "What do you say?"

Chapter Two

Hailey wasn't about to be taken in by a slick, fast-talking stranger.

If Detective Granger thought a badge gave his honor some kind of validation, he was mistaken. She wanted to boot him out the door, then sit at the window and watch him turn blue, although she wasn't entirely sure why. Partly because he was a cop.

But more than likely she was feeling testy because her plans to seduce Steven had run amok, and it seemed to be Nick Granger's fault.

"I'm hungry. And stranded." He slid her an easy smile, one she suspected was meant to disarm her anger and gain her trust. "If you have a spare blanket, I could sleep in the rental car."

She couldn't believe he'd suggest something so

stupid. Or was he playing on her sympathy? She couldn't be sure. "You'd be a human Popsicle before midnight."

"Does that mean you'll do the humane thing and offer me dinner and a place to sleep?"

Hailey glanced at the table she'd set especially for Steven. She'd had big plans for this evening—plans that didn't include a stranded detective.

Of course, she'd deal with her disappointment, as she'd long grown accustomed to doing, but did she want to offer lodging to a man she didn't know? A man she shouldn't find so darn attractive?

She wasn't afraid of Nick Granger, although she wasn't sure what made her think he was trustworthy. The fact that he was a cop? That part worked against him, although he probably didn't know it. Still, she couldn't very well send him out into a snowstorm with no place to go. "You can sleep on the sofa."

"Thanks. I'll get my bag out of the car."

She looked at the worn leather jacket he wore. It wasn't enough protection from the cold. "You get the roast out of the oven. I'll get your bag."

"You're not going outside in the storm. It's my stuff, I'll get it."

So his heroic side masked stupidity. She sighed heavily. "I've got a down-filled parka and boots. I doubt you'd make it back to the porch."

"I'm tougher than you obviously think," he said.

"And much bigger than me. I'd have a tough time dragging your dead weight back inside."

He flashed her a bad-boy grin. "Then leave me on the porch."

"Now that's an appealing thought, but it would prey on my sense of decency to let a defenseless stranger from sunny California freeze to death."

"That's one way to be rid of me."

She tossed him a naughty-girl smile, one she'd never perfected. "You're right, but it would probably draw a few Minnesota detectives to my house, and I'm not too fond of police officers."

Granger closed the distance between them and placed his hands on her shoulders. A sea-breezy scent, mingled with leather and musk, accosted her with his sexual presence. She found it tauntingly appealing yet unwelcome.

"You're not going outside." Those coffee-brown eyes settled on hers, stimulating her like an intravenous jolt of caffeine. His grip tightened—not in a threatening way but still rather convincingly. The detective was macho, it seemed. Too macho and bossy for her taste. Well, let him go outside and freeze his tush off.

In an effort to dismiss the arousing effect he had on her, she lifted her chin. "Have it your way. I'll put dinner on the table, and if you survive the ice and snow, wash your hands."

"I'll be back."

That's what Hailey was afraid of. She stood her ground until the door closed behind him.

Nick made it to the car, but it was colder than he'd anticipated—monstrously cold. He tried to think about the balmy weather back in San Diego, but it didn't help.

By the time he reached the porch, he was shivering so badly that he thought he'd never stop. When he opened the door and stepped inside the warmth of the small apartment-size house, he could see Hailey at work in the kitchen, and he expected her to say something to him.

Instead, she continued to wash tomatoes and leaves of romaine without looking up. She was a stubborn woman, so it seemed. The kind to serve a guy a good-size portion of hot tongue and cold shoulder when he didn't let her have her way. He glanced at his snow-covered pants and shoes.

The powdery stuff fell to the floor, and he realized a puddle of water would form on Hailey's hardwood entry. No need to set off Martha Stewart before dinner.

"Where…can…I…f-f-f-ind…a…t-t-t-owel?" he asked between chattering teeth.

"Oh, you made it back alive." She smiled sweetly, and her eyes glistened with feigned sincerity.

He didn't wait for an answer to his question, just joined her in the kitchen and snatched one of two dish towels from the oven door handle. He carried it back to the living room. By the time he had the floor nearly dry, she yelled, "Hey," jarring him from his task.

"What are you doing with my good towel?" she asked.

"Wiping the floor."

"Those are dish towels and they're only for looks. You're not supposed to use them."

"They were hanging in plain sight."

"That's a decorating touch. Like the curtains. I keep the regular towels in the righthand drawer."

If Nick weren't so hungry, he'd tell her what she could do with her towels. And since he needed to convince her to come to San Diego, he'd have to get on her good side. If she had one.

She opened the oven and stooped to pull out the roast. The backside of her was pretty nice.

Down, boy, he told himself. Wrong kind of woman. Totally wrong.

"It's ready," she said.

Nick noticed a bottle of Cabernet Sauvignon on the countertop. "Should I pour the wine?"

She shot him one of those lips-parted, taken-aback glances, like he'd suggested using Steven's toothbrush. Then her expression softened. "Sure. Go ahead."

He supposed drinking wine by candlelight made her feel uneasy, as if Nick was putting the moves on her, threatening poor Steven's position.

But that wasn't his intent. It just seemed a waste to let the bottle stay corked and lying on the countertop.

Besides, he thought, a grin tugging at one side of his lips, if he plied her with a bit of *vino,* she just might open up and tell him what she had against Harry. And Nick just might convince her to pack an overnight bag and fly back to California for the weekend.

Wham, bam, thank you ma'am—only without the sex.

Hailey, he noticed, prepared each plate before setting it at the table, a formality Nick wasn't used to. His idea of dinner was Chinese take-out or a couple of tacos.

Of course, there were those special meals at the Logans' house, but Harry's wife, Kay, always set the food out family-style, which seemed more like the way people should eat, if they were inclined to sit down with a napkin and silverware.

Nick had to admit the table Hailey had set looked inviting. He couldn't help wondering how a guy would go about getting seconds. Ask for them, maybe?

He poured the wine, then took the seat Hailey indicated was his. This was one woman who needed to loosen up, and he wondered if a bottle of Cabernet would be enough. "Do you want me to light the candles?"

She shot him another one of those you've-got-to-be-kidding looks, but strode to the kitchen and returned with a book of matches. Olsen's Bar and Grill, Mankato. Not that it mattered, but noticing details had become second nature to Nick.

He lit each wick, then watched the tiny flames reflect upon the crystal goblets, making them glisten with a romantic ambiance. He felt a bit guilty taking Steven's place, but not overly so. The conversation he meant to have with Hailey was better kept private. And intimate.

When she sat and primly scooted her chair forward, he lifted his glass in a toast. "To new friends and Mother Nature."

"To odd acquaintances and unfortunate twists of fate." She clinked her glass with his, then took a sip. Those baby blues studied him over the rim, and he couldn't help but wonder what she was thinking.

Hailey couldn't keep her eyes off the man who sat across from her, the stranger who had taken Steven's place at her table. She felt weird, as if she was cheating, which was crazy, since Steven had never suggested any kind of commitment.

Not yet, she corrected herself. The suggestion would have come tonight. She was sure of it.

She took another sip of wine and relished the warmth that slid down her throat, settling her nerves. And her conscience. As attractive and appealing as Nick Granger might be, he was definitely not husband material. She'd made up her mind to find a guy who was dependable. A real homebody who looked forward to weekends at the lake with his wife and kids.

A cop, no matter how good-looking, was the last person she would contemplate as a prospective life partner.

"Got a family?" He picked up a knife and began cutting his meat. "Brothers and sisters? Parents?"

The question surprised her, but she figured he was

just trying to make polite dinner conversation. ''No. Not anymore.''

There was so much she'd tried to forget, so much that was best left alone.

''What happened to them?'' He speared a slice of pot roast and popped it into his mouth. Still, those rich brown eyes studied her, awaiting her response.

Hailey fingered the stem of her glass, felt the cool, hard spindle of crystal that broke so easily if one wasn't careful when washing them. For a moment she considered telling him she didn't want to talk about it. But what did it matter? The guy was virtually a stranger and would be out of her life, once the storm let up. ''My mom passed away four years ago. I haven't seen my dad in years.''

''When did you last see him? Your dad, I mean.''

She wasn't sure why he was interested. Or why she bothered to even tell him. ''Twenty years ago.''

Her thoughts drifted to that cold, lonely night, the night her mother had cried herself to sleep for the first time Hailey had been aware of. The evening Harry Logan chose one family over another.

It had been the night before her sixth birthday, and Harry had come by to see her mother. They spoke privately in the kitchen, which they often did. When the adults came into the living room, her mom closed her eyes and pressed her lips together, as though trying hard not to cry.

''What's the matter?'' Hailey had asked.

Harry walked to the sofa, but didn't sit down. He

reached for Hailey's hand. "I can't come to your birthday party, honey."

"How come?"

Her mother's eyes welled up with tears. "Harry needs to spend more time with his wife and children."

Hailey hadn't known her father had another family. "When will we see you again?"

"I don't know, sweetheart." Harry bent down and gave Hailey a kiss on the forehead, then reached into his wallet and handed her mother a wad of bills.

"Do you think this is going to make everything okay?" Mama asked.

"Come on, Marilyn," Harry said. "I'm trying to do what's right."

"There's nothing right about any of this, Harry."

Mama cried after Harry left. Hailey cried, too. She hadn't understood what had happened. But she understood it now. And there was nothing Harry Logan could say to make her forget the pain his leaving had caused.

She took another drink of wine, only this time it didn't slide delicately down her throat. She choked, sputtered and coughed.

"You okay?" Nick looked at her with those coffee eyes, trying to be her best friend, she figured. Like two housewives who chatted about men and kids over a cup of the brew.

But Hailey wasn't about to dig deeper and tell this man stuff she'd buried long ago, stuff she wanted to stay buried. "I'm fine. It just went down the wrong pipe."

He flashed her a Brando grin, the kind a cop slid at a perp that had just backed himself into a corner. "Your old man must have really done a number on you and your mom."

"It was a long time ago. I got over it." She snagged a piece of meat with her fork and put it into her mouth, hoping that by chewing, she'd be unable to talk, and he'd take note of that.

"Twenty years ago you were just a kid."

Instead of answering, she jabbed a carrot.

"He must have run off with your candy," Nick said, a grin crinkling his eyes. "Or was it worse than that?"

"It was a lot worse." Hailey studied her plate, unwilling to look into those freshly brewed eyes that tempted her to bare her soul.

"He ever apologize?"

"Yes. Sort of."

"But you're not ready to forgive and forget?"

Hailey had a hard time forgetting a lot of things—her mother's broken spirit, for one. For all the mornings Hailey had to drag her mom out of bed, force her to eat a child-prepared breakfast, then encourage her to go to work so that the rent would be paid on time and groceries would be bought. "I've come to grips with the past. I don't hate my dad, but neither do I want to have a relationship with him."

"That's too bad."

"I'm doing fine on my own." And she was.

Hailey was the captain of her own ship, and her carefully laid plans guaranteed a life that was smooth sailing. Except for tonight.

As much as she wanted to avoid Nick's eyes, her gaze caught his and locked. Something passed between them, although she wasn't sure what it was. A kindred spirit kind of thing, it seemed. Like they had more in common than either would suspect. It momentarily warmed her heart, touched her soul. Whatever *it* was.

"What about you?" she asked. Lobbing the memories back in his court. "Do you have a family?"

"None to speak of, other than the cop who turned my life around. I was sixteen when I first met him. Back then I was a loudmouth kid who was angry at the world."

She studied the rugged, good-looking detective and tried to imagine him as a troubled teen. It was tough to do, because he seemed grown-up. Together. "Congratulations on the U-turn. You've obviously made some changes in your life."

"Thanks to a wise detective." He tossed her a crooked grin. "I'll never forget the first time I met him. It was Christmas Eve, and he caught me throwing rocks at a nativity display in Old Town."

"Did he haul you in?"

"Nope. He took me for a cup of hot cocoa at an all-night diner. Said he'd just gotten off duty and was hungry. We talked for a while. The next thing I knew, I was having Christmas dinner with his family." He flashed her a nostalgic smile, one that touched her heart with its sincerity. "I never knew what a real family was like, not until meeting them. And the fact is, I haven't been the same since."

"What about your own family? Didn't they miss you on Christmas?"

"My mom had already died. Fell down the stairs, at least that's what my stepdad told the cops. I guess they believed him, but I never did. Anyway, at that time I had no real place to call home, and no reason to celebrate the holidays." He scanned the living room, those stimulating eyes taking in each nook and corner. "You gonna have a Christmas tree?"

"Yes." She always did. In fact, she'd planned each and every holiday since Harry walked out of their lives. Her mom hadn't been up to the extra effort. It really wasn't so bad—taking over the household at an early age—because Hailey had come out on top. She was an organized dynamo at work and at home. Life ran smoother that way. No surprises.

Well, no surprises except the detective sitting across the table from her, but she'd grown adept at making the best of difficult situations.

They finished dinner with little conversation. Nick continued to refill their wineglasses until the bottle was empty. Hailey wasn't sure how they'd handle the bedtime stuff, but she was no longer uncomfortable with the good-looking detective in the house.

She wasn't entirely sure why. The wine maybe? The self-disclosures they'd shared?

Hailey didn't open up to people, especially strangers. She'd learned to keep her thoughts and feelings locked away inside—where they belonged, hidden with her memories and dreams.

The lights flickered once, twice, then went out altogether, leaving Hailey and the detective in the dark—except for the soft candlelight and the steady flames in the fireplace.

"Do you have any more candles?"

"In the bedroom."

He was heading down the hall before she realized she should have gotten them herself. She'd set the scene for romance in there, with aromatic candles glowing warmly throughout the room and the soft sound of love songs on the CD.

And in case that wasn't enough to give Steven a hint, she'd taken great care to make the bed look inviting.

Under the white, goose-down comforter that begged to be turned down, freshly laundered sheets with a light sprinkle of lavender scent awaited first-time lovers.

Maybe Nick wouldn't notice, wouldn't know what she'd planned for the evening. But instinct told her a guy like Nick wouldn't miss much. He'd have to be a dunce not to notice. And cops didn't get to be detectives by not being observant.

Maybe he'd be gentlemanly enough not to mention anything about her bedroom—or her obvious intentions.

A long, slow whistle told her he'd found the candles.

And that he wouldn't be a gentleman and keep quiet.

Hailey's heart sank low in her chest, and heat blasted her cheeks. She quickly stood and began to clear the table, wanting to keep herself busy so that she didn't have to look him in the eye when he returned from the bedroom, which now seemed like a den of iniquity, although she didn't know why.

She was a grown woman, for goodness sake, and could certainly spend a romantic evening with anyone she wanted. Where had the guilt come from?

Nick carried two candles into the living room and set them on the coffee table. "I guess the storm and I really screwed up your plans for the evening." Before returning to the bedroom for the other two candles, he chuckled. "I guess 'screwed up' was a bad choice of words."

She grimaced at his inappropriate attempt to joke and continued to wipe the table that no longer bore a crumb or a dribble. What she actually wanted to do was sling the dishcloth at him.

"Sorry," he said, as he reentered the room. "I guess that was out of line."

"My plans are none of your concern." She continued an overzealous attempt to scrub the table.

As he placed one of the candles on the mantel and the other on an end table, she blew out a ragged sigh. How was she going to manage spending an evening with this guy?

And what if they didn't clear the roads for days? If he were short and dowdy, instead of heartzappingly gorgeous, if he were quiet and shy—like Steven—instead of so quick with the snappy comments and sexual innuendoes, then maybe time would pass without a hitch. But as it was—

"I'm sorry, Hailey." His voice settled over her skin, like a blend of melted butter and warm maple syrup over a stack of hotcakes. And those freshly brewed coffee eyes offered a dose of compassion.

Coffee and hotcakes. Breakfast food. Another reminder this man would be spending the night.

She shrugged at the apology, hopefully brushing off thoughts of bedtime, rumpled sheets and morning.

He slowly made his way toward her and took the limp dishcloth from her hand, carelessly tossing it into the sink. She meant to reprimand him, and would have, had he not taken hold of her hand. His grip enveloped hers in a cocoon of warmth, and her skin tingled, her heart skipped a beat.

"I crashed into your life uninvited, and you served me one of the best dinners I've had in a long time. I'm sorry for teasing."

"It's okay." Her anger seemed to dissipate in the romantic ambiance she'd unwittingly set into motion. Yet she wasn't sure anything about this evening, this man or her growing attraction was even remotely *okay*.

He took the glass of wine she hadn't finished and handed it to her, then snagged his own.

"Come with me."

Chapter Three

Hailey's heart shot into overdrive. Was he going to put the moves on her, try to lead her down the hall and back into the bedroom?

If truth be told, she half hoped he would. Guys like Nick Granger had always appealed to her and made her common sense go haywire, but in spite of the arousing effect he had on her, she couldn't succumb to temptation. She wouldn't allow it.

Of course, that knowledge didn't do anything to slow a racing pulse or to still an incredible sense of anticipation.

He led her to the sofa. "Sit down."

"Why?" she asked, unable to quell the sense of seduction. And not just hers. She had half a notion to respond to each of his moves and make a few plays of her own.

Good grief. What was the matter with her? No way would she consider a one-night stand with a stranger. Yet when he flashed her another Brando smile, a part of her wanted his arms around her, his mouth on hers.

He motioned for her to sit, then took a seat on the other side of the sofa. His arm dangled over the backrest, but not close enough to touch. "Let's talk."

Talk? Was that part of the seduction? A line he used?

"Talk about what?" she asked.

"You. I want to hear more about little Hailey, the cute girl with pigtails and a missing tooth."

She glanced at the fireplace mantel, realizing he'd seen her photograph. As thoughts of Nick putting the moves on her flew out the window and escaped into the snowy night, a keen sense of relief mingled with disappointment. "There's not much to tell."

Nick studied the woman across from him, watched her struggle to open up. If he could piece together her life, understand her anger and disappointment, then convincing her to visit Harry in San Diego would be easier.

He was good at interrogating suspects, but this was different. Much different. A suspect's secrets were often a result of guilt. Hailey's secret was the result of a child's pain.

It was something Nick could relate to, he supposed.

She shot him a wistful smile. "My parents weren't married, and my dad was never really a part of my life. I suppose people don't really miss what they never had."

"I don't know about that." Nick still resented the sailor who'd fathered him, the man who'd refused to step up to the plate and be a dad. "It's been years, but I still blame my old man for the lousy stepdad I ended up with. And for the beatings I received just for being someone else's brat."

Compassion swept across her brow. "I'm sorry."

He hadn't meant to spill his guts like that, and he wasn't sure why he had. He supposed it was the wine, the quiet, introspective evening, or maybe it was something about the somber beauty sitting across from him. She continued to eye him with a tad more sympathy than he was comfortable with, blew out a slow, steady breath, then ran a hand through her long, brown locks of hair. The glow of the fire enhanced red and gold highlights he hadn't noticed before.

His fingers itched to touch the strands, but he removed his hand from the sofa back and dropped it in his lap.

He watched as she drew up her knees, tucked her feet under her skirt, and slowly turned to face him. "I did okay without a dad. It was my mom who took the brunt of his abandonment. She died loving my father, even though he dumped us both years ago."

Nick wanted to defend Harry, but didn't think it

was his place. If Hailey would just talk to the man, Harry could defend himself.

Twenty years ago, Hailey had been a kid. She couldn't possibly know the whole story. Hell, Nick didn't know the whole story, but he knew her father well enough to know there was something only Harry could explain.

Nick had never questioned Harry's values. The man was practically a saint. But even saints were human. Maybe Harry had tried to befriend Hailey's mom, like he had so many other people in recent years, and experienced a moment of indiscretion. And if the woman fell in love with him—

Hey, Nick had plenty of women look at him with hero worship. He just made it a point not to take any of them up on their various ways of showing gratitude. "Maybe your mom fell in love with your dad, but the feelings weren't mutual."

"Obviously not." Curled into the corner of the sofa, she looked like a small child. And Nick had a feeling that's where her thoughts were taking her— back to a sad childhood.

He had this sappy urge to go to her, offer her comfort and a shoulder to lean on, but God knew he wasn't that kind of guy. What did a man like him offer a woman who needed emotional support?

Hell, that huggy/feely stuff was learned as a kid, which was why Nick had never been comfortable with showing affection to anyone other than a lover. He'd never had the luxury of a hug or a pat on the shoulder, which were things kids needed. Women, too, he supposed. But it was a difficult gesture for him and another reason why he wasn't cut out to be a father or a husband.

She set her empty wineglass on the coffee table. He would have offered her a refill, but they'd finished the bottle. He could use another glass, too. The last swallow had left him warm and wanting.

Wanting more wine, he added. Of course, he wouldn't ask. When she rose from the sofa, he smiled, thinking he wouldn't have to.

He watched her go, but not to the kitchen. She padded down the hall and into her bedroom. He ached to follow her. Hold her close and chase the bad memories away. Give her some new ones.

Harry Logan might have convinced Nick to curb his delinquent ways, but no one had been able to shake the rebel from Nick's blood.

And the rebel in him wanted to follow pretty Hailey into the bedroom and offer her more than comfort.

Hailey didn't know why she knelt by the bed and reached underneath the dust ruffle for the old shoebox. She'd always kept the items hidden, even from her own sight. But for some reason she wanted to show the photograph to Nick.

She'd never confided in anyone before, other than a middle school teacher who'd sent Child Protective Services to visit their home. After that she'd kept quiet, kept things locked in her heart.

But tonight she felt the need to open up and share

the past with someone. To cry in her beer and confide in an understanding, tight-lipped bartender she would never see again.

And who better to share with than a man who would leave town as soon as the roads cleared?

She blew out a jagged breath and, resting her bottom on the heels of her feet, opened the box. A soft kiss of bittersweet nostalgia brushed across her heart, as she looked at the items her mother had treasured: a stack of letters tied with a faded pink ribbon. A couple of ticket stubs. A take-out menu from some diner in Florida.

In the midst of her mother's things sat something of hers. Something her father had given her after taking her to ride on a merry-go-round in the park.

She picked up the tissue-wrapped figurine and slowly unwound the paper, revealing a pretty, white carousel pony. In spite of herself, she fingered the cool ceramic, studied the colorful reds, blues and yellows. At one time she'd wanted to throw it away or break it against the wall. But she hadn't. Instead, she'd stashed it inside her mother's box, which was a good place for it, she supposed.

After wrapping the tissue around the pony and putting it back into the box, she withdrew what she'd been looking for—the old photograph her mom had blown up from a strip of black-and-white pictures taken at the drugstore in Florida, where they used to live. She looked at it closely for a moment, then replaced the lid and slid the box back where it had been, out of sight but rarely out of mind.

When she returned to the living room, the soft glow of the candles and firelight gave the room a mystical iridescence. Magical. And, she supposed, sensual, if what they were sharing had been physical.

She handed Nick the black-and-white photo, then sat beside him, closer than she'd been before. With the new level of intimacy they'd reached, sitting near enough to touch seemed appropriate.

He took the picture, and as he did so, his fingers grazed her hand. Her breath caught, and her heart paused before going back into a strong, steady beat.

As he studied the only photograph she had of her parents, a lump formed in her throat. Funny thing about crying, she supposed. Years could go by without shedding a tear, and then the floodgates threatened at the weirdest times.

"Your mom looked a lot like you. Pretty. Same expressive eyes. You take after her." He didn't comment about her father, which was all right with her.

"They had it taken in one of those little booths at the five-and-dime. They're both smiling like crazy kids. Happy, you know. It was one of my mom's most cherished possessions."

"But not something you cherished," he said. "You don't keep it on the mantel with the other pictures."

He was right. She didn't place any sentimental value on the photograph or any of the other stuff her mom had saved. She wasn't sure why she kept any of it, since the box of memories was a solid reminder of her mother's descent into depression.

Hailey supposed it was a cop's job to notice the little things and make assessments. "I stashed the picture in a shoebox full of my mother's personal belongings that I keep under the bed."

"What else do you have in that box?"

A pretty pony my father gave me, after taking me to the park to ride the carousel. But she didn't see any point in mentioning it to Nick. "Just a few letters my dad sent my mom, some of which contained cash—never a check. I think she would have kept the money as a memento, but we had a hard time making ends meet."

"I'm sorry."

Hailey figured he meant it, that he'd, at least on some level, had plenty of disappointments in his own life. Maybe that's why she found it so easy to confide in him. "I'd always considered my dad a hero because he was a policeman. And I looked forward to every visit."

Nick nodded as though he understood, but she wasn't sure he really did.

"I could never understand why he didn't live with us, like other fathers did, but I figured it was because he was busy. I didn't know he had another family." Hailey sighed softly, again recalling the painful night she'd seen her father for the last time.

He'd promised to come to her birthday, and she'd told all of her friends they could meet him. But something had come up, he'd told her, and he couldn't come to her party the next day. Then he'd handed her a twenty-dollar bill, as though the money would appease her. It hadn't.

She looked at Nick, caught him watching her, waiting for her to speak. "The night before I turned six, he and my mother had an argument in the kitchen. I'm still not entirely sure what it was about, but my mother spent the night crying. The next morning she got a wild hair, and we moved to Minnesota."

"Just like that?" Nick asked.

She wasn't sure what he meant.

"Did your mother leave a forwarding address? Any way for your dad to find you?"

"I don't know. Maybe not." Hailey bit her lip until it hurt. She supposed that might be one reason Harry had neglected to call until just two weeks ago. But he was a cop, a detective, and he'd found her in Walden, hadn't he?

"Maybe it was your mom's fault he wasn't there for you."

"In part, maybe." She blew out a sigh. "But my mom still suffered from his rejection. She had good days and bad ones. Sometimes, during low points, she used to drink—Scotch and too much of it. One day, when I was about ten, I came home from school and found her passed out on the bed. She was clutching that photo in her hand."

"People get sentimental when they drink to forget."

"Yeah, I suppose they do. But mom had an empty bottle of sleeping pills on the nightstand." The tears

Hailey had fought began to well in her eyes. "I called 911."

"Tough job for a kid."

"Yes. But at least help arrived in time." She paused. "*That* day."

"That day?"

"Four years ago, I came home too late. I called the paramedics, and they called for the coroner." A sob escaped from someplace where it had lain dormant for years, and the man across from her reached out his arms.

Hailey had never had someone to hold her, to offer comfort. And as much as she wanted to maintain an emotional distance, she fell easily into his embrace.

Nick held Hailey while she cried, stroking her back. Her hair, clean and silky, sluiced through his fingers. The scent of lilac encompassed him, wrapping him in a swirl of softness.

He'd never held someone so gentle, so vulnerable in his life. And he wasn't sure what he should say. Something sappy, probably. But he couldn't bring himself to utter a word. His hands just moved up and down her back, as though they knew instinctively what to do, how to comfort. The rest of him didn't have a clue.

Her sweet touch stirred his blood, aroused an erection he tried to ignore. Sexual feelings, he supposed, were the only ones he was adept at handling.

Something mushy in his heart went out to Hailey—both the child who'd had to deal with a suicidal mother and the young woman who'd blamed her dad for the misery in her life.

Harry had told Nick there was a lot more to the story than met the eye. And Nick had no trouble believing him. Harry wasn't the kind of guy to father a child and not acknowledge her. He was too decent. Too moral and upstanding.

Nick considered telling Hailey who had sent him and why, but thought better of it. Too much had been said tonight. He'd wait and discuss it over coffee in the morning.

When Hailey's tears had been spent, she pulled away and swiped at her eyes with the back of a hand—first one, then the other.

"I'm sorry," she said, sniffling again and offering him a weak smile. "I don't usually get weepy."

He cupped her cheek, his thumb brushing against the softness of her skin. "It's been a tough evening."

"Yeah," she said, again wiping her eyes. "And it's time to call it a night. I'll get you some bedding for the sofa."

When she stood, her eyes remained locked on his. And as she moved, her shin rammed the glass edge of the coffee table. "Ouch."

"Are you okay?" Nick reached for her hand, pulling her gently around. He stooped to look at her leg, taking the shapely calf in his hand.

"I'm fine," she said. "Really."

But something in her eyes told him she wasn't fine. And neither was he. But it had little to do with pain from contact with the table, and everything to do with the heat of his touch.

When he stood, facing her again, she swallowed hard, and her lips parted.

Damn. He had an incredible urge to kiss her. Just once.

She must have had the very same fantasy, because she placed a hand on his shoulder, then moved her fingertips toward his neck, his jaw, his cheek.

Ah, Hailey. Nick was lost in her touch, in her springtime scent.

He pulled her close and lowered his mouth to hers. She moaned in anticipation, or maybe surrender. He wasn't sure, but when she opened her mouth, allowing his tongue to seek hers, the rebel in him took over.

The kiss was deep and hot. Demanding. And Nick couldn't seem to get enough of the woman in his arms. His hands roamed her back, her hips, and he pulled her flush against him. Against a telltale erection. If he'd frightened her, she gave him no clue, because she only leaned in closer.

He didn't know where this was heading. The decent side of him said to back off, but the rebel side wasn't listening.

When Hailey placed her hands against his chest and broke the kiss, he wasn't sure whether he felt relief or frustration. Probably a combination of both.

"I'm sorry about that," she said.

"About the kiss? Or about stopping it?"

"Both, I guess." She offered him a half smile, as

though trying to shrug off the obvious desire they'd both shared, but a passion-induced flush on her chest and neck told him her arousal would take longer to subside than her words suggested.

"Yeah. Me, too," the decent side of him said.

"If you'll excuse me, I'll go get the bedding for you." She drew away, leaving him with the lingering scent of lilac.

While she disappeared down the hall to a linen closet, Nick plopped down in the easy chair and sank back into his seat. The evening had taken a lot out of him, but it wasn't just the spilling of tears and memories that had affected him. Something else had zapped the energy out of him, weakened him like he'd stayed in a sauna too damn long. He'd never been that close to an emotional woman before. At least not one that wasn't yelling and throwing things at him.

He stood when Hailey entered the room and helped her make up a bed on the sofa, but they both remained quiet. Lost in their thoughts.

And their regrets, he supposed, although he didn't regret the kiss. Not really. His real regret was the damn erection that continued to plague him.

She glanced down at the bed they'd made, then looked up at him and smiled. "Good night."

"Night." He stood there for a while, long after she took one of the candles, padded down the hall and closed the bedroom door.

He figured sleep would be a long time coming, but

he slipped out of his pants and draped them over the easy chair in the corner.

Usually, he slept in the raw, but tonight, as he settled onto the sofa, he figured it best to wear his briefs.

Hours later the flame in the fireplace had dwindled down to a soft red glow, and although he was tired, sleep evaded him. He stared at the ceiling and continued to contemplate the woman who slept down the hall.

When a scream sounded from behind the closed bedroom door, he jumped from the sofa.

''No!'' Hailey shrieked.

A nightmare or an intruder?

He flung off the blanket and rushed down the hall, ready to battle whoever or whatever had frightened her.

Chapter Four

Nick threw open the bedroom door, only to find Hailey sitting upright in bed.

Alone.

No intruder.

A candle flickered on the dresser, bathing the room in soft, muted light. And the scent of lilac and lavender filled the air.

She wore a white satin nightgown with tiny straps that outlined near-perfect breasts. Her hair, rumpled from sleep, tumbled over her shoulders and down her back. She looked ready to cry.

And in need of comfort.

Don't get too close, the rebel in him warned. What the hell do you know about comforting women? Turn around and go back into the living room.

But the decent side of him stepped forward, leading him closer to the bed. "Are you okay?"

"I guess so." A tear welled in her eye, then ran down her cheek. She swiped it away. "Did I scream?"

He nodded. "Yeah."

"I'm sorry." She blew out a shaky little breath. "I had a nightmare."

Talking about the past had probably triggered it.

Nick felt a bit guilty for prodding her to reveal those memories, for his part in creating the demons that plagued her sleep. Lord knew he'd had his own share of night demons.

If he was lucky, he had a woman beside him, because sex usually took his mind off his troubles—at least momentarily. But he wasn't about to suggest that to Hailey.

Still, the thought seemed to hang in the air. But he wouldn't go there. Not without a push.

Her eyes scanned the length of him, halting when she reached his waist.

Oh, cripes. He was only wearing his shorts. Now what? Did he turn around, go back into the living room and grab his pants? Or ignore the fact he was practically naked. And damn-near-fully aroused.

Maybe he should act like comforting distressed women was no big deal. Just all in a night's work.

His feet seemed rooted to the hardwood floor, but a streak of decency commanded his voice. "I, uh…had a gut reaction to your scream. I didn't take time to put on my pants."

"It's all right," she said. "I'm sorry for scaring you."

Yeah, she'd scared him. Initially. But now his blood-pumping reaction was caused by the sight of her sitting in the midst of a rumpled bed, a whisper of white satin draped over nipples that seemed more pronounced as the seconds ticked.

Nick had always been partial to those satiny fabrics on women. He liked the way slinky material slipped through his hands, slid along the skin. His heart pounded like a runaway steam engine, even though there was no longer a chance of physical threat.

And there was only one place his blood seemed to be coursing. Could she see his erection? Sense the sexual awareness that zapped through the room like a Fourth of July fireworks display?

Hoping to dispel the star-spangled, sensual aura, he said, "I thought someone broke in."

"I'm okay."

Yeah, well he wasn't.

Shoot. The initial adrenaline rush from her scream had long since been replaced by an unwelcome case of desire.

"I'm sorry for waking you. Will you be able to go back to sleep?" she asked.

"I doubt it." But not because of the adrenaline. Testosterone was a bigger problem right now. Of course, he wasn't going to let his hormones take over. He and Hailey were both adults. They didn't need to act on their desire. Or acknowledge it.

"Want to talk for a while? To get your mind off the nightmare?" Nick asked, trying to be a nice guy, even though he didn't feel like much of one right now.

She nodded, then scooted over, making room for him. "Yes, I'd like that. Thanks."

The mattress sank, as he sat on the edge of the bed. In an effort to give himself something decent to do, he flipped the switch of the bedside lamp, but nothing happened. "Electricity is still off."

Hailey ran a hand through the strands of her hair. "I've got plenty of candles. Do you want more light?"

Heck, no. He liked the soft, sexy glow of the candle burning by her bedside. But the candlelight, among other things, was doing a real number on the nice-guy persona he was trying to tap into. More light would be better, he supposed. But maybe he should toss the decision back in her lap. "Whatever you're comfortable with is fine with me."

He'd better think of something else to chase the desire away. Something to get his mind off white-satin-draped breasts and nipples begging to be touched. Something to get his mind off a demanding erection.

"I haven't had that dream in a long time," she said. "But it always leaves me feeling frightened and alone. I can't explain it."

"You've had it before?"

She nodded. "And it's always the same scenario. I'm a kid. The sun is going down, and the house is getting dark. I can't find my mom. Then the wild dogs or coyotes start howling until they shriek like banshees. And then something starts scratching at the door.''

He suspected she was still dealing with feeling abandoned, but what the hell did he know about dreams and their meanings?

''You're safe, honey.'' He placed a hand on her jaw, and his thumb caressed her cheek. ''It was just a dream.''

She leaned into him, and in a move that seemed perfectly natural, he wrapped an arm around her and gave her a comforting hug.

Hailey slipped easily into Nick's embrace and rested her face against his lightly bristled cheek. She inhaled the scent of man and musk, relished the feel of her breasts against his chest, the beat of his heart against hers.

Never had she felt so safe, so alive. So aware of herself as a woman.

As wrong as this might be, she held him close so he couldn't release her before she'd had enough time in his arms.

Enough time for what?

Her body wasn't craving comfort any longer, but something more. Something a school librarian concerned about her reputation had no business thinking about.

But maybe she shouldn't think. Maybe she should only enjoy the feel of the handsome man in her arms.

The memory of the hot kiss they'd shared earlier

in the evening came crashing to the forefront. The kiss that had set her blood boiling and her body yearning for fulfillment.

Maybe she needed to forget about the little girl who'd been left alone, the organized woman dead-set on landing the perfect husband, the school librarian who wouldn't dream of inviting a strange man into her home or her bedroom.

Unable to help herself, she nuzzled his cheek, placed a kiss along his jaw. Heaven help her, she wanted more than comfort. A lot more.

Nick moaned, as though struggling with his own thoughts and feelings, fighting his own temptation, then turned and caught her lips with his.

He slid his tongue inside her mouth, kissing her like she'd never been kissed before, promising something she'd never experienced and wasn't likely to ever have again.

The kiss deepened, and raw need took over. Hands explored, stroked, caressed. Breaths mingled, and heat exploded in a sexual rush.

If Hailey had any reservations about making love with a man she would never see again, her apprehension quickly dissipated in the sexually charged room. She'd never been so fully aroused or felt so wanting.

Never had a lover made her feel so powerful, so special. So desired.

She was unable—and unwilling—to stop the runaway passion, the mind-robbing assault of her senses.

There was no turning back. She lifted her nightgown and slipped it over her head, to allow more skin-to-skin contact, to feel Nick's flesh against hers. She wanted him. Badly. And nothing else seemed to matter.

He loved her with his hands, his mouth. Slowly, as though savoring each touch, each kiss, each flick of the tongue, he drove her wild with need.

And when he finally entered her, she was lost in a storm of overwhelming desire and hunger. She arched to meet each thrust, until they reached a mind-shattering, body-shuddering climax.

As the last wave of pleasure passed, they both lay still, quietly hanging on to each other as though afraid to move, to break the tenuous connection between them.

As Nick held Hailey in his arms, still amazed at the climax they'd shared, his mind began to clear. And he realized how careless they'd been.

Where were those damn condoms she'd bought?

He rolled to the side, taking her with him. "I...uh...we forgot to use any protection."

Her eyes widened, as though her brains had left town, too. "It's in the drawer."

"Yeah, well they're not going to do us any good in there." A heavy sense of guilt washed over him. Why hadn't he been more thoughtful? More responsible?

Because he hadn't been thinking about anything other than how much he wanted to have sex with Hailey. About how damn good it felt to run his hands along her skin, to kiss her, to bury himself deep within her.

But his brain was finally starting to kick in. And so was his conscience. "I hope we didn't make a big mistake."

"I think it will be okay," she said. "I'm due to start…well, you know. I just bought the condoms to be on the safe side. I don't normally do this—"

"I don't normally do this without being careful." Nick didn't want to ponder how stupid he'd been. "Do you want me to go back to the living room now?"

"Not unless you really want to. But if you wouldn't mind staying the rest of the night, or at least until I fall asleep, it wouldn't feel like a…"

Her words trailed off, but he knew what she meant. If he held her during the night, it wouldn't feel like a one-night stand, even though that's exactly what it had been.

"Long-distance relationships don't work very well," he said to make her feel better about what they'd done. But the fact was Nick wasn't too good at making a relationship work, no matter where a woman lived.

He kissed her cheek and held her close, which, for some crazy reason, felt like the right thing to do. Maybe the gesture would make up for not using his head before letting his libido take over.

Hopefully, the best sex he'd ever had wouldn't come back to haunt him later.

One way or another.

Nick, who didn't normally have any qualms about having sex without a commitment, had just made love to Harry's daughter, a woman he'd meant to befriend. A nester who wanted more out of life than he was prepared to offer anyone.

And as Hailey snuggled against him for the rest of the night, regret settled in for a long winter's stay.

Hailey woke to sunlight pouring through her window and the sound of her doorbell, but when she tried to throw off the white, goose-down comforter and climb from bed, an arm and a broad shoulder held her down.

Nick.

She'd asked him to sleep with her. And apparently he'd taken her up on the offer. Slipping out from under him, she climbed from the bed, snagged her robe from the closet, stepped into a pair of slippers and padded down the hall to the front door.

Her mouth nearly dropped to the floor when she spotted Steven on her front porch. He was bundled in a red parka with a hood, a bright-yellow muffler, blue mittens and a pair of black galoshes. A bit on the chubby side, anyway, the rosy-cheeked accountant looked like one of those blowup balloon figures used in the Macy's parade.

She pulled the edges of her robe together at the neck, trying to hide the fact she wore nothing underneath. "Hi, Steven."

"Roads cleared earlier this morning," he said, offering her a shy smile.

"Good." She looked over her shoulder, hoping that Nick didn't come wandering down the hall.

"You got company?" Steven nodded toward the snow-covered rental car in her drive.

"Uh, yeah."

"Well, I won't keep you, then. Looks like I woke you up." He glanced at his watch. "Nearly noon. I thought you were an early bird."

"I didn't sleep well," she said, although she'd slept great, once Nick had joined her in bed.

"Just wanted to let you know that I was sorry about not making it last night. I'd stayed late at the office, trying to finish an audit I was preparing for a firm."

"I understand," Hailey said, wanting to rush him off before Nick sauntered into the room and complicated things.

"I got to visit my mother, though." Steven flashed her a grin. "She lives in Mankato, and since I couldn't make it home, I stayed there. Mom invited the gal who lives next door over for the evening. And we all ate popcorn and watched a movie."

Under normal circumstances, Hailey might have asked about the "gal" who lived next door, gotten an age or description of her. But right now, it didn't seem to matter whether Steven's mother was doing a bit of matchmaking or not.

Hailey's relationship with her neighbor—what there was of one—had hit a brick wall. At least for the time being.

Hailey wouldn't be asking Steven to dinner again

anytime soon. Switching gears—or men—didn't come that easy to her. And even if it did, something told her poor Steven would pale in comparison to Nick Granger.

"I'm glad you had a nice evening," she told the accountant. "Maybe you and I can try dinner another night."

"Okay." Steven adjusted his glasses on the bridge of his nose. "Let me know when. You're a good cook."

"Thanks." Hailey didn't wait for him to step off the porch before closing the door.

Why did she feel guilty? It's not as though she and Steven had more than a neighborly relationship at this point. He'd never even kissed her, although she suspected he'd wanted to. Once.

But she felt like a cheat, just the same.

By giving herself to a stranger, she'd cheated herself. Cheated herself of the dreams she had, the plans to have a stable family and loving husband.

And Nick wasn't merely a stranger. He lived clear across the country from her. And worse, he was a cop. There wasn't anything about him that made for a stable relationship.

Other than the best sex she'd ever had.

She'd told Nick not to worry about forgetting to use the condoms. And she *was* due to start her period. But as a woman who always prepared for the unexpected, pregnancy weighed heavily on her mind. How could she have been so caught up in the heat of the moment that she'd neglected to use birth control?

"Who was at the door?" Nick asked from the hall.

She turned to face him, saw him wearing only a towel—another reminder of the intimacy they'd shared. "No one in particular."

Now why had she lied? Why not just tell him it was her neighbor?

Because Nick knew exactly what she'd planned for last night—a premeditated sexual romp with Steven. And she didn't want to bring up the subject, didn't want to even think about it.

"Did Steven say the roads were clear?"

So, Nick knew—or assumed, with his cop's intuition—who she'd been talking to.

She crossed her arms and leaned her weight on one foot. "How long have you been listening?"

He shrugged and slid her a Brando smile. "Not long."

"I guess you'll be leaving, then." She tried to conjure a smile, tried to ignore the memory of hot sex that lingered in the air. Tried to distance herself from the man who'd taken her to a place she'd never been before last night.

"I'd like to shower first." He raked a hand through sleep-tousled hair. "And talk to you about a few things."

About the future? she wondered.

What future? Whatever they'd shared was over. Done. Gone with the storm that ended as quickly as it had struck.

Hailey hoped Nick wasn't trying to make this into more than it was. She was a big girl and knew better than to pin her dreams on one passion-filled night. There was so much more to life than that. So much more to her hopes and plans. "You don't need to talk to me about anything, Detective."

"Yes, I do." He snatched his pants from the chair he'd draped them over last night. "After I take a shower."

Nick had meant to talk to Hailey as soon as he dressed, but she insisted on showering after him. As it was, he'd finished two cups of coffee while waiting for her to join him.

It was just as well, he suspected. Figuring out how to tell her about Harry was going to be tough, especially since making love had really complicated things.

He glanced at his watch. What took women so damn long in there?

Ten minutes later Hailey strode into the kitchen looking like a morning-after dream come true.

She'd clipped her hair into a twist of some kind. Her cheeks bore a natural color, but she'd applied a light coat of lipstick. Even dressed casually in a pair of faded jeans and an oversize white sweatshirt, he found her prettier than he had last night.

"Coffee?" he asked, while leaning against the counter.

"I'll get it."

As she poured a cup of the brew and doctored it

with sugar and cream, Nick tried to find the right words to broach the subject he'd put off too damn long.

"Remember when I told you that I came to Minnesota looking for someone?"

She nodded, then removed the spoon from her cup, took a sip and studied him over the rim.

"Harry Logan is a good friend of mine."

Her mouth dropped, and the coffee splashed as she set the cup on the countertop. "Why didn't you tell me?"

"Harry said you'd hung up on him when he called you a week or so ago. And I figured you had your own side of the story. I was afraid you'd throw me out before I got a chance to speak on his behalf."

"Don't waste your time, Detective." She crossed her arms and leaned against the counter. "I have no intention of having a relationship with Harry Logan."

"I understand that. If I were you, I'd be mad, too."

"Oh, yeah?" she asked, voice raising. "I've got plenty of anger to spread around. If you think last night worked in your favor—"

Nick stepped across the kitchen and took hold of her arm, clutching just tightly enough to make a point. "Now just one minute. Let's get something clear, honey. Last night happened because we were both too damned hot for each other. If I'd had the ability to think clearly, we wouldn't have forgotten the condoms."

Her gaze lanced his, and she swallowed hard. Even this morning, with voices raised and emotions ripped apart, the sexual chemistry was still there, ready to explode.

He released her—with reluctance. "Last night, as good as it was, had absolutely nothing to do with any of this."

She opened her mouth to speak, as though she intended to argue, to put up a fight. About what, he couldn't be sure. Then she clamped her lips tight.

The truth of their powerful attraction, he supposed, left little to dispute.

"I'd like you to come to San Diego with me," he said. "Can you take some time off work?"

"No, Detective Granger. I'm not going anywhere. I have to work on Monday and won't get any time off until Christmas break. But I don't intend to waste my vacation on Harry Logan."

"You must not know Harry very well. He's one of the greatest guys in the world."

"I know Harry as well as I need to," she said, taking a sip of her coffee. "As far as I'm concerned, he gives the term *deadbeat dad* a whole new meaning."

Nick understood her feelings. But if she would just give Harry a chance, the guy could explain. "I'm sure there's more to the story than you know."

"Maybe so," she said. "My mom would certainly agree with your assessment of the man. She died loving Harry Logan in spite of his abandonment."

"Harry lost track of you, Hailey. He wants to make things right."

"He's wasting his time. That man may be my biological dad, but he means nothing to me."

"I'm sorry to hear that," Nick said. "Harry was the father I never had."

"Oh, yeah?" Hailey said, her voice laden with sarcasm. "Harry was the father I never had, too."

Nick kept his mouth shut, unsure of how to respond to that. The scars she carried ran deep. And there didn't appear to be much he could say to convince the stubborn woman to give a guy a second chance to prove himself.

It seemed pretty clear that his mission had been a failure. He'd just have to return to San Diego with his tail between his legs and tell Harry he'd had no luck in convincing Hailey to travel with him. The rest of his guilt—sleeping with his friend's daughter—would remain a secret. Even a rebel had a conscience.

Nick blew out a sigh and decided to try one last route to Hailey's heart. "Harry would have come himself, but he's in the hospital."

The hospital? Hailey bit her lip. Did it matter that that the man was sick or injured? Did it make things any different?

She didn't wish Harry Logan any harm, she just didn't want to be a part of his life. Or let him be a part of hers. He'd had his chance years ago. He hadn't acknowledged her as his daughter then, choosing his real family over her.

And that was okay. She'd grown up just fine without a dad. And she certainly didn't need one now.

"I'll send him a get-well card. I'm afraid that's the best I can do."

Nick nodded slowly. "Well, if your mind is made up, then I guess there's no reason for me to wait around here any longer."

"No, there isn't." Her heart thumped against the wall of her chest, but she stood tall. She and Nick Granger had no future together. And the sooner he left, the sooner she could try to get her life back on track.

He walked to the living room window and peered out into the driveway. "Do you have a shovel I can use? The car is buried fender deep."

She gave him the snow shovel, then tried to keep herself busy, tried not to watch his efforts to clear a path to the road.

When he returned, he had built up a sweat, as well as a shiver. And his jeans were wet to the knees. "Can I use your bathroom before taking off? I'd like to change my pants."

"Sure."

Her bittersweet emotions seemed to tumble around inside. She wasn't sure what she was feeling, other than a hodgepodge. But she felt sorrow, for sure, mingled with a bit of relief.

When he had finished in the bathroom, he returned to the living room where she stood, giving her a soft kiss on the cheek, a kiss that made her chest ache and her eyes water.

"Take care, Hailey."

She nodded. "You, too."

He hesitated a moment, as though he wanted to say something, then he turned and quietly walked out the front door.

She watched out the window as he climbed into his car and drove away. She wanted to scream out, to be angry with Nick, although she couldn't seem to figure out why. Maybe it was because of his tie to Harry. Maybe he was just a handy target for her disappointment in the man who had abandoned her mom.

But more likely it was because he taunted her with something she'd never wanted, something she would never have.

Tears that seemed to come from nowhere poured down her cheeks, and she went into the bathroom to find a tissue.

What she spotted first was one of her good towels—the one Nick had used—skewed to the left and hanging unevenly. Without contemplating why, she lifted the fluffy, embroidered towel to her nose and tried to catch one last whiff of the man who'd shared her bed.

Then she placed the towel back where it belonged, making sure it hung straight beside the other. Trying, she supposed, to put her bathroom and, hopefully, her life back in order.

God willing and the creek didn't rise, her biggest worry wouldn't come to pass.

What in the world would she do if she and Nick had conceived a baby last night?

Chapter Five

Three weeks later Hailey stood in the bathroom and stared at the home pregnancy test on the white tile countertop. She'd driven all the way to Granville to purchase the darn thing, just so no one would recognize her.

But if her suspicion proved true, she'd have a hard time keeping things a secret or maintaining an upstanding reputation at Walden Elementary or in the community.

She peered at the plastic stick that rested in its stand and prayed that the telltale pink dot wouldn't appear. But as she watched in slow, steady anguish, a pale circle began to form until it blazed bright, like a neon sign.

Hailey's heart—and her hopes—sank low in her chest, and she blew out a ragged breath.

Pregnant.

In spite of her plans to provide a loving, two-parent home for her future children, Hailey would have a baby out of wedlock. How could she have been so stupid? So swept up in desire that she'd had unprotected sex with a virtual stranger?

She was pregnant with Nick Granger's baby.

Now what?

Did she try to locate the detective in San Diego? Tell him he was going to be a father? Or keep that precious secret under lock and key?

What, if anything, should she tell the man who had merely been a one-night lover? The man who didn't at all seem like her idea of a daddy?

Time, she decided, would be her best ally. She needed to think and plan, to come to grips with such a life-changing situation and map out a new future.

But time didn't seem to be on her side.

Several days later, on a cold Saturday morning during Christmas break, the phone rang while Hailey decorated the small Scotch pine she'd placed near her living room window. She released the garland of artificial cranberries she held in her hand, letting it dangle to the hardwood floor. Then she snatched the phone that rested on the end table—a handcrafted antique she'd found at a flea market in Mankato. "Hello."

When Nick's gravelly voice sounded over the line,

her breath caught, and her heart slipped into over-drive.

"How have you been?" he asked.

She gripped the receiver tight, as though he might sense her hands had grown moist from the lie she was about to tell. She would tell him she was doing just fine, even though she wasn't. She was pregnant. And unmarried.

Tell him about the baby, her conscience pleaded.

Not yet, her heart countered.

She needed more time to consider the ramifications of involving Nick Granger in her life. In her baby's life.

Of course, that was assuming he would even give a hoot about the child they'd created. "I'm fine, Nick. How about you?"

"I'm okay," he said. "But...Harry isn't. He's going to have a quadruple bypass tomorrow or the next day, depending on some test they're running."

Hailey didn't answer right away. She'd made it clear to Nick how she felt about having any kind of relationship with her father, but the seriousness of Harry's pending open-heart surgery poked at her conscience.

"I thought you might want to reconsider coming out to see him." Nick blew a weary sigh into the phone. "You know, just in case..."

He didn't have to finish the words. Hailey knew what he meant. It was one thing to say she didn't ever want to see Harry again, to vow not to have any kind of relationship with him. And another thing to know she might never have an opportunity to change her mind, if there were complications with the procedure.

She glanced at the brass clock on the mantel. It was nearly noon. Could she even get a flight out of Minneapolis this late in the day?

"I'll see what I can do," she said.

"You'll come to San Diego?" Nick asked, as though wanting a firmer commitment.

She couldn't give him one. Who knew what the flight schedules and seat availability would be like this close to Christmas? "Give me a number where I can reach you. I'll let you know if I can purchase a ticket."

After giving her his cell phone number and hanging up, Nick blew out a heavy breath.

For weeks he'd felt like a jerk for not bringing Hailey home to see Harry. Sure, the retired detective had accepted the explanation Nick had given him— that Hailey had stubbornly refused to return—but it hadn't assuaged the guilt Nick carried for having slept with his friend's daughter.

He paced the living room of his downtown loft apartment, a spacious, one-room home with no walls—the perfect place for a don't-fence-me-in kind of guy.

Surely she could snag a ticket. He strode to the window that overlooked the city, watched the miniature cars poke along the busy street, the little pedestrians zipping in and out of shops and restaurants. Everyone, it seemed, had a place to go. A job to do.

Everyone but Harry, who'd been in the hospital for weeks while doctors tried to stabilize him for the surgery.

When the cell phone finally rang, he quickly answered. "Granger."

"It's me. Hailey. I've got a seat on a flight arriving in San Diego at ten tonight."

Relief poured over him as some of the guilt he'd been harboring eased. "That's great. I'll pick you up at the airport."

She didn't respond, and he figured she might prefer to call a cab instead. But he would put up a hell of an argument. Getting Hailey to see Harry was Nick's responsibility. And this was one mission he intended to see through, even if it meant keeping Hailey under his wing until she got a chance to talk to her dad.

"All right," she said. "I'll be on Northern Air flight number 413."

He scratched down the information, all the while feeling a growing sense of satisfaction. Contentment.

Excitement, too, he supposed. He tossed aside the fact that he might want to see the pretty woman again, and clung to something far more important.

Now he could make up for his earlier failure. He could hand deliver Hailey to her father.

Flight 413 took off an hour late from Minneapolis and, after bypassing a thunderstorm over the Rockies, lost even more time while in the air.

Hailey adjusted her watch, rolling it back two

hours, yet her body still insisted it was past her bed-time, and she was eager to get settled into a motel room for the night. Nick said he'd pick her up, and she wondered where to look for him.

Near baggage claim, probably. Or maybe at the curb.

He wouldn't have to wait much longer, since the only luggage she'd packed was a black canvas carry-on that held everything she would need for the two days she planned to remain in town.

All she wanted to do was meet with Harry and have him offer some sort of explanation for the past. She'd accept her father's apology with a smile and let him face his surgery in peace.

Then she'd leave San Diego and head back home. Of course, she'd wait until after he came out of recovery before flying back to Minnesota, which seemed like something a dutiful daughter would do.

When the plane pulled to a stop at the gate, she grabbed her canvas tote from the overhead bin and waited for what seemed like forever to disembark. Then she followed the throng of passengers heading for baggage claim and ground transportation. Her steps slowed when she spotted Nick standing with arms crossed near the security checkpoint.

In spite of Hailey's resolve to keep the detective at arm's distance, to pretend nothing had ever hap-pened between them, her heart skipped a beat at the sight of him, then it ricocheted in her chest like a pinball in motion.

Wearing a pair of faded jeans, a white T-shirt, the

familiar aviator jacket and the hint of a smile, the rugged detective reminded her of an undercover cop who could easily carry himself as a streetwise thug.

Had he portrayed a bad guy in the past? Was his job just as dangerous as the glimmer in his eye?

As his gaze zeroed in on her, following her down the escalator, she forced her sluggish feet to pick up the pace until she reached him.

As much as she hated to admit it, she'd missed his bad-boy smile, his gravelly voice. His arousing touch. Why was she always attracted to the men who were wrong for her? And why this particular man?

No matter how hard she'd tried to forget the night of passion they'd shared, she couldn't. It was etched too deeply in her mind.

And, unfortunately, the fact that she was carrying a lifetime reminder of that evening wouldn't allow a convenient case of amnesia to set in.

He brushed a kiss on her cheek, which surprised her, then took her bag. "Thanks for coming."

She didn't respond right away. What was she supposed to say? You're welcome? I wouldn't miss my father's surgery?

Unable to come up with anything better, she said, "I'm sorry you had to wait."

"No problem. It's too late to go by the hospital tonight, so I'll take you home. We can see Harry tomorrow morning." He took her arm and guided her up the escalator that led to ground transportation and short-term parking.

I'll take you home?

Hailey didn't think staying at Nick's house was a good idea. Not with what they'd shared in the past hovering over them. Or at least over her.

Every time she glanced at his profile, caught the determination and intensity in his gaze, she was reminded of the passion that raged in his soul. The desire he'd released in hers.

Hailey wasn't at all ready to face the stimulation she received from those caffeine-laden eyes. She needed a good night's rest if she planned to see Harry tomorrow morning. And sleeping under the same roof as Nick Granger promised to keep her up all night long, thinking, remembering. Wanting.

No, going to his house wasn't a good idea.

"You can just drop me off at a motel along the way," she said.

"Nothing doing. You're going to be my guest."

Stay with Nick? The guy who stimulated her senses even now?

No, she shouldn't stay with him. Why let temptation have another shot at her? Yet pride wouldn't let her admit her real concern. "I don't want to put you out."

"You're not putting me out." His tone of voice and determined step implied an argument would be useless. "Besides, I owe you one. It's my turn to provide you room and board."

More than a little tired from the long and unexpected trip, Hailey didn't feel like butting heads. What the heck, she told herself. It would only be for a night. Two at the most. Surely she could put aside her attraction and keep a level head for that long.

Besides, she really shouldn't spend any extra money on a hotel room. This last-minute flight had cost a bundle, and her savings account had taken a good-size hit. With the baby coming, she would need to save every penny she could.

Again her conscience stirred, and she questioned whether she should tell Nick about her pregnancy or not.

Not yet, she decided. But she would take him up on the offer to stay with him. Hopefully, sharing a home with the father of her baby for a day or two wouldn't complicate things between them any further.

He led her across the parking lot until they came to his car, a late-model, black Jeep Wrangler. She didn't know what she expected him to drive, but the all-terrain vehicle seemed to fit his personality. Something sporty for a man comfortable with the outdoors.

After Nick backed out of the stall and exited the terminal, he turned on the radio to a late-night jazz station, which was nice, since Hailey wasn't up for a discussion or polite chitchat. She preferred to keep her thoughts and feelings to herself.

So she sat back in the leather passenger's seat and tried to enjoy the sights and sounds of the harbor town at night, as well as the view of a multitude of ships docked along the wharf to her right.

San Diego was a pretty city, an interesting place

for a tourist to visit, Hailey decided, although she doubted she'd ever come back.

Minutes later Nick pulled into a private underground parking garage that required a card to activate the wrought-iron gate and parked in his allotted space.

The building seemed to be safe and secure, but Hailey's pulse raced in apprehension as they entered the elevator that took them to the highest floor. Alone. At the top of the world.

Nick unlocked his door and let her enter the loft apartment he called home.

A pair of pants covered the back of a reclining chair, and an empty long-neck beer bottle perched on top of the wide-screen television. In the far corner, next to a bike and a set of golf clubs, he'd propped a surfboard upright, its rubber leash curled on the floor.

The walls, white and stark, waited patiently for a decorator's touch, while a stack of dishes in the sink begged for a maid's attention.

Hailey didn't know what she expected, but apparently the rugged detective hadn't gone to any extra effort for her arrival.

"Interesting place you have here," she said, thinking a comment was in order.

"It works for me. I'm not home very often."

She made her way to the window overlooking the city that displayed a magical panorama of bright lights that created an impressive skyline.

"Pretty view." It was the most positive statement she could make about his male domain.

Nick stepped behind her and placed two hands on her shoulders. The heat of his touch sent her heart racing, her blood surging. He gently steered first her body, then her eyes to the west. "Look over there."

With his spearmint-tinged breath against her hair, his musky scent accosting her senses and his hands warming her shoulders, she had to fight the urge to turn from the window and face the man who stirred more than a memory. But reason prevailed, and she maintained a tenuous grip on self-control.

She followed his instruction and caught a narrow glimpse of the harbor that glistened in the moonlight. It was breathtaking.

Or was it Nick's touch that caused her wired reaction?

How could a man so out of sync with her idea of a dream mate stir more than memories of their lovemaking?

Instead of the stunning view or the mindless reaction she had to his touch, or the memory that begged for a repeat performance, she tried to focus on their differences. The reason why a long-distance relationship with a man like Nick wouldn't work.

Stepping away from his touch and his sea-breezy scent, she tried to conjure up an unaffected smile. "You have a beautiful view and an interesting home."

"Thank you."

"I'm not sure what kind of sleeping arrangements you've got in mind, but I'll take the sofa."

Nick studied the pretty brunette who appeared so out of place in his loft apartment. A woman who turned him inside out whenever he looked at her, whenever he remembered being in her arms, in her bed.

But making love to Harry's daughter once was enough to convince him that no matter how attractive he found her, no matter how much he wanted to give her a lover's welcome-home kiss, Hailey Conway was strictly off-limits.

His battered conscience wouldn't allow an instant replay of their last night together. No matter how great it had been.

"I'll let you have the bed," he said. "And I'll take the sofa."

She glanced across the room to the screen that blocked the king-size bed from the rest of the house. The screen that Carla had purchased and left behind when she'd moved out.

His once-upon-a-time, live-in lover hadn't liked the one-room place. She'd been insisting upon a home in the suburbs before the last fiery argument had ended their two-month relationship. Nick figured Hailey, too, might be concerned about privacy. "The bathroom door locks."

She wandered toward the bed and peeked around the screen.

"Sheets are clean," he added, figuring that would matter to her.

She nodded. "Thanks."

For changing the sheets? Or for not pressing that they sleep together in a bed big enough for two? He wasn't sure.

The bedtime stuff was going to be tough. Especially with the memory of the hot, snowy night spent in Hailey's arms. Never had a past sexual encounter affected him with such longing. Or such guilt.

"Do you mind if I turn in?" she asked. "It's two hours later in Minnesota. And I'm sleepy."

"Not at all. We need to get up early and head for the hospital."

She nodded, then took her black tote bag to the bathroom to do whatever women did in there.

He heard the door lock.

After snatching a spare blanket from the built-in cabinet by the bathroom and taking one of the pillows from the bed, Nick made himself a place to sleep on the couch and lay down—fully clothed, this time. He wasn't about to take any chances that Hailey's memories were just as strong as his, that she felt just as aroused as he did.

He glanced at the bathroom door, wondering what she'd wear to bed tonight. The satin nightie she'd had on last time?

Minutes later, when she stepped out of the bathroom wearing a pair of men's flannel pants, an oversize T-shirt and socks, his curiosity was sated.

Apparently, she'd chosen something safe. But if she could read his mind, she'd know the excess material hadn't steered his thoughts away from sex. Because Nick already knew—firsthand—the perfect body that lay just beyond the cotton and flannel. Beyond his reach, he reminded himself.

Which was too damn bad.

For him, anyway.

But there was no room in Nick Granger's life for a woman like Hailey, and the sooner he got that idea ingrained in his mind, the better.

He rolled to his side and faced the large picture window, studied the starry sky and the bright city lights. Looking at anything but the flimsy screen that separated him from Hailey.

It was going to be a long, sleepless night.

Chapter Six

Nick hadn't slept more than an hour or two all night. He'd counted sheep, plumped his pillow a hundred different ways and just plain watched the clock on the cable TV box, to no avail.

No matter how hard he tried, he couldn't keep his mind off the pretty woman who slept in his bed. But in spite of the memories of their last night together, he'd managed to keep his libido in check.

His temporary roommate, on the other hand, had dozed like there was no tomorrow.

Just before dawn, Nick had finally thrown in the towel, deciding to start the day with a shower. Then he walked down to the corner to pick up the news-paper and purchase a large cup of coffee. When he returned, he tried to be quiet. Of course, his efforts hadn't been necessary.

Hailey, it seemed, was dead to the world.

Or at least oblivious to him and the haunting night of passion they'd spent in each other's arms.

The sun had finally begun to creep above the mountains in the east, where the sky was streaked with muted colors of pink and orange, and Nick grew eager to get Hailey to the hospital before a horde of Harry's family and supporters arrived to maintain a vigil at his bedside.

Nick wanted her visit with her dad to be as low-key and as private as possible. The two had a lot of ground to cover, and not much time to do so.

Poking his head around the screen that offered very little privacy, Nick saw the petite young woman tucked into his bed, dark hair splayed on the pillow. A flannel-covered leg peeked out from the covers, offering him a glimpse of skin and revealing a small bare foot and toes trimmed with pink polish.

Unwilling to gawk like an adolescent voyeur, he stepped back behind the screen and cleared his voice. "Good morning. It's time to get up."

He heard her roll over and mumble something. Then the sheets rustled as she climbed from bed. He watched as she wandered away from the screen and into the bathroom, sleepy-eyed, hair tousled and a pair of fuzzy slippers on her feet.

The toilet flushed, water ran in the bathroom sink. And then silence.

Get a grip, he told himself. Find something to do

other than dwell on the woman who'd warmed his bed while he flip-flopped on the couch like a grunion on the moonlit shore.

When Hailey returned several minutes later, her hair had been combed.

"Where do you hide the clean towels?" she asked.

"In the closet to your right." He studied her over the rim of the plastic foam cup that held his morning brew. "There's a great coffee bar and newsstand on the corner. Want me to get you something to drink while you shower?"

"Tea, if you don't mind. Coffee hasn't been sitting well on my stomach lately." She tucked a strand of hair behind her ear and offered a shy smile. "Thank you."

He nodded, but didn't make a move for the door. Instead he merely gazed at the woman who looked as sexy as hell in baggy, plaid flannel pants, a University of Minnesota T-shirt and a pair of pink fluffy slippers.

Cripes, he had the urge to take her back to bed. Or to suggest they shower together.

But they had something more important to do, and he was eager to get moving. Eager to take Hailey to see her father and to offer his support to Kay while Harry went under the knife. "Will it take you long to get dressed?"

"Is fifteen minutes too long?"

Nick glanced at his watch, then caught Hailey's eye. "Fifteen minutes is fine. I'll go downstairs and get your tea."

"Do you have a piece of toast to go with it?" she asked.

"I'll see what I can rustle up."

When Hailey stepped into the bathroom, Nick strode to the kitchen area to look for some bread. It had been a long time since he'd made a sandwich, but he remembered buying a loaf a while back. Was it this week? Or last?

He found the bread on top of the fridge. But when he pulled the plastic bag down and looked inside, he chucked the whole kit and caboodle into the trash. He didn't suppose Hailey needed a year's worth of penicillin toasted. Maybe he'd better pick up a sweet roll or croissant at the coffee bar.

Fifteen minutes later, Nick returned with a cup of tea and a brown bag holding a bagel and cream cheese only to find Hailey waiting for him.

Fresh from the shower, she wore a pair of jeans and a cream-colored sweater. With cheeks flushed, dark hair shimmering, lips looking downright kissable with a light rosy gloss, she appeared ready to go. The only thing missing was a smile.

"Nervous?" he asked.

"A little." She wiped her hands against her denim-clad hips, indicating she was more than a little apprehensive.

"Harry's a great guy," Nick said, trying to reassure her. "And he's really looking forward to seeing you."

She grabbed her black purse and slipped the

leather strap over her shoulder. "It's not Harry I'm worried about."

Her comment took him aback, but only for a moment. The entire Logan family would show up at the hospital today, along with most of the guys Harry had taken under his wing—guys like Nick, who owed the old man a hell of a lot more than words of condolence and support.

And Hailey, whether either of them liked it or not, would be subject to everyone's scrutiny.

"I was the product of an affair," she reminded him. "Now that Harry's looking mortality in the eye, he'd like to see me and appease his conscience. But I doubt the others in his family will feel the same."

"Kay and Harry have a hell of a marriage. But I guess there was a time when things were kind of rocky."

"Obviously," she said.

But Hailey didn't know the Logans. Not like Nick did. He wasn't sure what kind of reception she'd get, but he doubted anyone would be rude or treat her badly. They'd been far too accepting and forgiving of too many hard-ass delinquents in the past.

Why not one young woman who would only be in town for a day or so? A woman who hadn't asked to be born?

"Kay and the boys won't hold anything against you, honey."

The sappy endearment had slipped out, surprising him, but Hailey didn't appear to notice—thank goodness.

She glanced at her wristwatch, a delicate gold bangle, then báck at him. "Let's get this over with."

"All right." He opened the door for her. "Come on."

As they left the building, Nick had the urge to slip an arm around her, but he shoved his hands in the front pockets of his jeans instead.

He might have told Hailey that Kay and the boys would welcome her. But that had been his gut talking, his conscience begging her not to back off or change her mind. Emotions would be running high at Oceana General Hospital today, and he wasn't exactly sure how anyone, other than Harry, would react to seeing the young woman who'd been born out of wedlock.

But Nick would be there for Hailey.

Whatever that might be worth.

Perched on a hilltop that overlooked the Pacific, Oceana General Hospital was located about twenty minutes north of downtown San Diego. The large white building had an old-world, Spanish style, with a flower-lined walkway and a stone-crafted water fountain bubbling at the entrance.

As Nick walked stoically at her side, Hailey entered the glass doors that opened to the lobby with robotic steps, moist palms and a queasy stomach.

Runaway nerves plagued her unmercifully, and a little girl's voice urged her to duck and hide…to insist Nick take her back to the airport. But she braced herself for the meeting she'd agreed to.

Nick led her to the elevator and up to the fourth floor. He'd obviously come to visit Harry many times.

Hailey's tennies squeaked along the tiled corridor as they approached the nurses' desk, announcing their arrival. A pretty blond RN glanced up and slid Nick a friendly smile.

He nodded. "Good morning, Mary. How's he doing?"

"I don't think he slept very well. And he was up early this morning." The attractive nurse flashed the detective an appreciative gaze, then turned to Hailey.

Nick made a quick introduction, explaining that Hailey was Harry's daughter.

"Nice to meet you," the woman said. "You have a wonderful father and a great family."

As far as Hailey was concerned, she had no father and no family, but she managed a weak smile. "Thank you."

The cordial response was part of the game plan, part of the act. She would grant Harry the forgiveness he wanted, then head back to Minnesota where she belonged.

"Come on," Nick said, taking her arm and leading her to Room 436. "I'll wait outside."

"You're not going in with me?" she asked, her voice sounding too much like that of a frightened little girl.

"No."

Nick opened the door, then with his hand placed against her back, gently urged her inside the small hospital room where an older man lay in bed, his eyes on the door. His eyes on her.

"Hailey," he said, his voice soft yet gruff. A warm smile spread across his wrinkled face. "I'm glad you came."

She tried to return the smile—and maybe she did—but her emotions were all balled up inside.

Seeing Harry—once strong and vibrant, now bed-ridden and pale—struck a sympathetic cord and seemed to ease some of the anger and resentment she'd harbored in the past.

"Hello, Harry." She made her way closer to the bed, pausing a couple feet away.

He appeared older, a bit tattered and worn, and not anything like the tall, powerfully built man who had lifted her on his shoulders to point out a bird's nest in the backyard. And his blue eyes, she noted, weren't nearly as bright and vivid as when he'd shown her the hero's medal the mayor had awarded him for bravery in the line of duty.

Hailey may not have seen Harry Logan in nearly twenty years, but she didn't need familiarity to spot a wan complexion and realize his health was shaky— at best.

For some reason she wanted to tell him it was okay, that he didn't need to worry about explanations or excuses. But she figured he needed to bare his soul.

And as much as she hated to admit it, she was more than a little curious to hear what he had to say, what reason he would give for walking out of her life, for breaking her mom's heart and spirit.

"You're so pretty. Just like your mother."

Hailey stiffened for a moment, then relaxed. Her mother had been an attractive woman. Broken, but pretty, when she managed to comb her hair and smile.

"Thank you."

"I'm glad you came," Harry said. "There's a lot I want to tell you, so much I need to explain."

Hailey wanted to wave him off, to tell him she'd grown up fine without a father, without him. That the past was over and done. No hard feelings. She'd trained herself to accept her lot in life without dwelling on the pain or disappointment. Isn't that what she was doing now? Going through the motions? Allowing Harry a chance to absolve himself of guilt?

She took a seat by his bed and pressed her lips together, letting him do the talking. The apologizing. The explaining. She would merely accept his apology, whether she could actually do so or not.

"I met your mother during a low point in my life," Harry said. "Kay, my wife, had left me and taken Stevie, Danny and Joey with her. I was lonely. And hurting."

So Hailey hadn't been the result of a sleazy affair. She supposed that was a bit of a comfort—the fact that Harry was somewhat free to court her mom before leaving her pregnant and alone.

"I cared about your mother. A lot." Harry's eyes beseeched Hailey to understand. "She offered me comfort and friendship when I was lonely and missing my boys something fierce.''

Hailey thought of the black-and-white photo taken at the five-and-dime. Grief washed over her, just as it did whenever she pulled the old photograph out from the box under her bed and studied it.

''I have a picture of you two,'' she told Harry, ''taken at one of those little photo booths. You were both smiling.''

''I remember. We were in Florida. That's where we used to live, where I met your mom.'' The memory brightened the blue flecks in his eyes. ''It was Christmas, and the holidays had done a number on me. I had some vacation time, so your mom suggested we drive down to the Keys. We stopped at an amusement park along the beach. I forgot the name.''

Surfside Park. Hailey hadn't forgotten; her mom had spoken of the trip and the place often enough. But she doubted the sentimental stuff would mean much to Harry, so she didn't respond.

''After your mother and I returned, Kay approached me about a reconciliation.'' His gaze snagged hers, and his expression grew serious, somber. ''You gotta understand, Hailey, I had three boys to think about. And I didn't know your mom was pregnant. She hadn't told me.''

A stab of guilt shot through Hailey as she thought about Nick, about her own pregnancy and the urge to keep her condition a secret.

Had her mom faced a similar dilemma, had some

of the same worries and concerns? Considered the same options?

"Your mom was pretty broken up about our split," Harry said, "but she seemed to understand. When I called her a week later, just to check on her, to ask how she was doing, her phone had been disconnected. She'd left town without talking to me. I'm not sure whether she knew or suspected she was pregnant at the time. But either way, I didn't know."

His sincerity was hard to ignore, and Hailey found herself believing him.

"Kay and I thought we needed to make a fresh start, so about six months later, I accepted a job with the San Diego Police Department, and we moved the family out here."

If her mom had taken off without telling him where she was going, and if he moved shortly thereafter, it was no wonder that Harry hadn't been a part of Hailey's early years. But there was more to the story than that.

Hailey still held the vivid memories of a six-year-old to prove it.

"I remember you coming to visit," she said. And the doughnuts you would bring. The smile that lit Mama's face whenever your patrol car pulled into the drive.

"About seven years after your mom and I split, after Kay and I reconciled, I got a call down at the station. Your mom had traced me to San Diego. She told me about you and hoped that I would consider a relationship with you both."

Had the call upset him? Had he wanted to start things where he and her mom had left off?

A hundred questions swirled in her mind—probably too many for Harry to answer. Had he agreed to continue the relationship with her mother? Or had he gotten angry at the woman who had dared to disrupt his life? Had he been happy to learn he had a daughter? Or had he refused to take responsibility?

Had they fought? Accused each other? Pointed fingers and dealt out blame?

Only one question proved important enough to surface: How did you feel when you learned you had a daughter? Or more specifically: How did you feel about *me?*

But Hailey was afraid to voice it, to throw her heart on the table. Instead she tweaked the question into one that wouldn't make her appear so vulnerable. "Did you believe her? About me being yours?"

Warmth glimmered in Harry's eyes, and his mouth quirked into a half smile. "We went through the motions of a blood test, but I didn't need the DNA results to tell me you were my little girl. Your mom had never lied to me. And I'd been her first lover."

Her mom's *only* lover, Hailey suspected, since she never remembered another man in her mom's life.

"In my heart I knew you were mine. Besides, you looked just like my kid sister. You still do," he added with a smile. "Only prettier."

"Thank you," she said, wondering if she would ever meet the woman who was her aunt. In spite of her reluctance to get involved with Harry, curiosity niggled at her.

"I wanted a relationship with you, Hailey. I swear I did. But Kay, my wife, had just been diagnosed with breast cancer. She was facing surgery, as well as chemo. I didn't want to cause her any additional stress. I couldn't chance telling Kay about you. Not then."

Nick had said there was a lot Hailey didn't know. This, she supposed, was one complication she hadn't considered. "Does your wife know about me now?"

"Yes," Harry said. "And she's looking forward to meeting you."

That seemed unusual. And awkward, at best. Hailey wasn't sure she wanted to meet the woman Harry had chosen over her mom.

"My wife is a wonderful person. You'll like her."

Hailey merely nodded, unwilling to send the man to face bypass surgery without any hope that things would be okay.

But things weren't really okay—not as far as Hailey was concerned. She might have a better understanding of the past, of the adult relationships that had touched her life as a child. But she still harbored painful memories. Resentment.

"You missed my birthday party," she said, unable to leave a child's disappointment behind.

"Kay was going into the hospital for a mastectomy that day. I had to be there with her."

Life, Hailey realized, was more complicated than a child could comprehend. And sometimes more complex than an adult wanted it to be. The anger she'd held on to for so long began to dissipate, although she still didn't welcome a complete reconciliation with her dad. Too much had happened, too much time had passed.

Hailey's life was on track in Minnesota—well, at least it had been before the pregnancy.

"Shortly after Kay's surgery, your mom took off again. And she didn't leave a forwarding address. It took me years to find you."

"And when you did find me, I didn't want to talk to you," Hailey supplied, taking on a bit of guilt herself.

"I understood, honey. You were just a kid, and I'd let you down. You had every right to be mad." He slid her a gentle grin. "But you're here, now. And that's all that matters."

She looked at the man lying in the hospital bed and caught the hope in his eyes. Unable to help herself, she reached out and took his hand in hers. "Yes, I'm here."

A dark-haired nurse, older and not nearly as attractive as the blonde, entered the room. "Mr. Logan, I need to take some more blood."

"I'll slip out for a while," Hailey said, eager to get some fresh air, to have some time alone. Time to think and sort things through.

"Will you come back?" Harry asked.

"Yes. And I'll be here during the surgery." Then she gave her father's hand a gentle squeeze, before walking out of his hospital room.

Her chances of finding time alone dwindled the moment she spotted Nick standing in the midst of several men, all roughly his age, and an attractive rosy-cheeked woman with copper-colored hair.

Nick turned, and before Hailey could slip off or excuse herself, he introduced her to Kay Logan.

Harry's wife extended a hand in greeting. "It's nice to finally meet you, Hailey."

Was it? Hailey found that difficult to believe. But she caught a glimpse of sincerity in the woman's eyes. And something else, although she couldn't quite put her finger on what it was.

"It's nice to meet you, too," Hailey said, hoping her words sounded half as truthful as Kay's had. Her stomach turned topsy-turvy, and she feared she would be sick—right here in the hospital corridor.

Good grief. She'd give anything to make a fast exit before she embarrassed herself.

The soft-spoken woman cast her a warm smile. "I'd like to talk to you, if that's all right. Would you care to join me for a cup of coffee in the cafeteria?"

Coffee? Just the two of them?

Hailey looked at Nick, hoping for a lifeline of sorts. An excuse of some kind.

"Go on," Nick said, offering her no help at all. Then he told Kay, "I can come get you if the doctor shows up while you're gone."

Hailey's stomach knotted, and nausea surged with a vengeance.

"I don't drink coffee anymore," was the only excuse she could muster.

"Then have tea. Or juice," Nick supplied.

Hailey wanted to kick him in the shins. But she took a deep breath and slowly let it ebb from her lungs. "Sure. Why not?"

Then she allowed Harry's wife to lead her down the hall and to the elevator.

Hailey sat across the small cafeteria table from Kay Logan, a cup of tea in front of her.

"I'm glad you came out for the surgery," the older woman said. "It means so much to Harry."

Her gracious response took Hailey aback. She wasn't sure what she'd expected from Harry's wife, questions about her mother, she supposed. Harsh words, maybe. A turned-up nose. But certainly not warmth or kindness.

"I don't plan to stay long, just a day or two." Hailey took a sip of the tea, hoping it would soothe her stomach.

It didn't.

"I understand."

Did she? Hailey wasn't sure, but there was a good reason why she wanted to rush home. And not just because of an upcoming neighborhood holiday party and the end of Christmas vacation.

Hailey Conway didn't belong here—in California, with her father's real family.

"Harry wanted to talk to you before the surgery. He's carried a lot of guilt for years." Kay's eyes glistened with what appeared to be unshed tears. "I think that's one of the reasons he worked so hard to reach some of the boys he befriended. He wasn't able to be a dad to you, so he fathered troubled youth instead.''

Hailey noticed a small gold cross that hung from a delicate chain around the older woman's neck. Was she a woman of faith? Was that what Hailey had noticed? A loving heart? A gentle spirit?

For some reason, Hailey felt free to speak. "I've been angry at Harry for a long time, but there was a lot I didn't understand.''

"Harry would like to be a part of your life, if you'll let him.''

Hailey didn't know about that. A quick visit was one thing, but she wasn't ready to make any changes in her life. She needed time to regroup. It was all too much, too fast, too soon.

Unable to give Kay an answer until she thought things through carefully, Hailey said, "I'm happy living in Minnesota.''

"I understand. Maybe you can come out for a visit from time to time.'' Kay studied her over the rim of her coffee mug, then smiled warmly. "It's amazing. You look a lot like our oldest son. Steven. Your eyes are the same shade of blue.''

Hailey looked like her half brother? Did they both look like Harry's sister? Their aunt?

Again curiosity raised its head. "Will Steven be here today?''

"No,'' Kay said, her voice strangely hoarse. "He died in a helicopter accident during Desert Storm.''

"I'm sorry,'' Hailey said.

"Me, too."

They sat quietly for a while, each of them lost in their thoughts.

Harry's wife wasn't at all what Hailey expected and she couldn't help commenting. "I'm surprised you've been so accepting of me, of this situation."

"Oh, I had my moments," Kay admitted. "It isn't every day a woman finds out her husband has a child by another woman. It took some getting used to. And a bit of prayer."

Hailey thought it might take a bit of tears, too. Maybe a dish thrown across the room. Angry words. She was unable to quell her curiosity, not only about Kay's reaction, but Harry's.

How had he felt, learning of Hailey's birth? Had he been upset? What had happened when he leveled with his wife?

"When did Harry tell you about me?" Hailey asked.

"About ten years ago. And I must admit, I was mad as an old wet hen." Kay smiled, then fingered the gold cross that rested on her pink sweater. "But not for the reason you might suspect."

"Why, then?" Hailey asked, wanting to know, to understand.

"For him not telling me sooner." Kay lifted her cup and took a sip. "I understood why he didn't want me to know about you while I was fighting breast cancer. But he waited several years, and he shouldn't have kept you a secret."

"How did you take it?" Hailey asked. "When he finally told you."

"It's not as though Harry cheated on me," Kay said. "I'd asked him to move out. I'd made the decision to end our marriage. I was young, and I couldn't handle the worry of his dangerous job, the hours he was away from home. The stress. In a way, I drove him to your mother's arms."

"What made you change your mind? What made you want to make the marriage work?" Hailey asked.

Again Kay fingered her necklace. "God spoke to my heart. I realized that I'd made a mistake, that I'd taken the easy way out. My boys needed their father. And quite frankly, I needed Harry, too. I loved him. And the separation convinced me that I didn't want to be alone."

Hailey nodded.

"After our reconciliation," Kay said, "we made a promise to each other not to keep any secrets. Not to let the sun go down on our anger. To make each day count. Like I said, he should have told me sooner. It was something we should have faced together. As a team."

Before Hailey could speak, a man walked by with a tray loaded with sausage and eggs. The spicy aroma rose off the plate and accosted Hailey, causing a gag reflex. She slapped a hand over her mouth and dashed to the ladies' room.

She barely made it.

Once inside a stall, she wretched violently until

she'd lost the tea and bagel she'd had earlier and. didn't stop until she'd expelled a bellyful of yellow bile.

A nervous stomach?

Somehow, she didn't think so. The nausea, she feared, was her first bout of real morning sickness.

"Are you okay, dear?" Kay said from behind the bathroom partition.

Hailey wiped her face and mouth with a wad of toilet paper. "I'm fine. Really."

"Are you ill?" the woman asked.

No. Somehow, Hailey knew she wasn't sick. Thank goodness. But what kind of excuse could she give?

"I'm allergic to eggs and sausage," she responded. "Just the sight of it makes me sick."

The excuse sounded lame, even to her. But hopefully Harry's wife believed her.

"Would you like me to ask Nick to take you home?" Kay asked.

"No!" Hailey snapped, then she caught herself and lowered her voice, gentled her tone. "There's no need to call Nick. I'll be just fine."

Leaving the hospital sounded like a great idea.

But having Nick Granger hear about her morning nausea was the last thing in the world Hailey wanted.

Chapter Seven

Nick chatted with Harry until one of the nurses, Mary, came in and said it was time for Harry's shower.

"I'll wait in the hall," Nick said, before slipping out of his old friend's room.

He'd always been uneasy in hospitals—maybe because he'd seen enough people suffer here, die here. Victims, perps. Each time he entered the E.R. doors and caught the medicinal smell, he was reminded of human frailty, vulnerability. But Harry's plight had forced him to toughen up, or at least show up often enough to know the fourth-floor nursing staff by name.

Hell, who was Nick to complain about being here?

Poor Harry had been cooped up in this place for weeks. And visiting him was the least Nick could do.

In the designated waiting area located by the nurses' station, Nick watched for Hailey and Kay to return. He chatted for a while with the middle-aged woman in 412 who took her daily walk with an IV pole connected to her arm. Her name was Marge, and she'd been here nearly a week.

As Marge started her second lap, Nick spotted Hailey and Kay striding down the hall, side by side.

Kay wore a pleasant smile, but Hailey appeared wan and kind of puny. Maybe the school librarian disliked hospitals as much as Nick did. But more likely, meeting Harry and Kay had been stressful for her.

It was, undoubtedly, time for a break. He supposed they could both use some fresh air and sunshine.

"I'm so glad we had a chance to meet," Kay told Hailey. "And I hope you feel better."

Feel better? Was she sick? Nick wondered.

Hailey offered Harry's wife a smile. "I feel better already, thanks."

Not sick, then, just uneasy. He could certainly understand that.

"If you'll excuse us," Nick told Kay, "I'd like to take Hailey out for a ride. She hasn't had a chance to see much of San Diego, and she'll soon be heading back to snow country and the land of ten thousand frozen lakes."

"There's no need for either of you to hang out

here," Harry's wife said. "I'll give you a call when I find out the specifics on the surgery."

Nick brushed a kiss upon Kay's cheek. "Thanks. We'll be back." Then he took Hailey by the hand and led her out of the hospital.

For a moment he thought she might pull away, but she held on tight and kept up with his brisk pace.

"Are we going home?" she asked. "I mean back to your place?"

"No. I thought I'd take you to Bayside. It's an oceanfront community about ten miles from here."

Fifteen minutes later Nick turned down Bayside Drive and drove to the public parking lot a short distance from the sand. He didn't tell her that Bayside was the city where Harry and Kay lived. He'd simply chosen this spot for the ocean view and the shops that lined Tidal Way, a little street that ran along the shore.

They climbed from the car, and Nick took a moment to savor the sea breeze, catch the fresh, salty air. To gaze at the expansive ocean and the blue, cloudless sky.

Nick loved the beach. He thrived on the peace and respite he found whenever he watched the waves splash upon the sand or searched the horizon that stretched as far as one could see.

"It's so pretty here," Hailey said.

"Yeah." Nick followed her gaze beyond the breakers, where two Hobie Cats sailed alongside each other. "I don't get much time to myself, not with my job. But when I do have a day off, I like to come here.''

Hailey looked his way, casting him a gentle smile. When the breeze whipped a strand of hair across her face, she tucked it behind an ear. ''I haven't lived by the beach in a long time, not since I was a child. And that was just for a month or two. I guess my mom followed Harry to San Diego with the hope that he'd…''

She didn't finish, didn't need to.

Nick reached out, cupped her cheek. ''I hope things work out between you and your dad.''

She shrugged, then turned toward the shore. ''It doesn't matter.''

Nick figured it did, much more than she let on. But he let the subject drop. He'd never been comfortable with facing emotions head-on. But so what? He'd found life was easier that way. And he sure as hell couldn't fault Hailey for skirting the emotional junk, too.

The sunshine and sea breeze—and maybe the peaceful setting—had put some color back in her cheeks. Her blue eyes fairly sparkled.

With the pretty brunette in the foreground, he couldn't help but appreciate the view more than before and found himself gawking at her.

And remembering…

Candles burning low. The scent of lavender. Brown hair splayed upon the white pillow. Bedroom eyes glazed with desire. The immense pleasure he'd found in her arms.

His gut tightened as he remembered her mouth on his. On him. Her tongue…

Heaven help him, he wanted her all over again.

But he'd better banish crazy ideas like those. There was a slew of reasons he and Hailey couldn't be more than friends at best—the least of which was their respective relationships to Harry. But even if Nick's mentor and friend gave his blessing to their ill-fated union, it wouldn't work. Hailey was a nester. And Nick Granger didn't need a house for much more than a place to hang his clothes.

He loved his freedom, appreciated the ability to come home without listening to someone nagging him about leaving the toilet lid up, for squeezing the tube of toothpaste in the middle or for drinking milk right out of the jug. Why was that such a big deal, anyway?

It had been Carla, a nester like Hailey, who'd taught him to value his freedom.

After nearly two months, Carla had hightailed it out of his place, leaving only the stupid screen by the bed and a couple bottles of cleaning products under the sink—products Nick refused to use on principle alone, he supposed.

But it was his place. His life. And he didn't need anyone trying to make him into something he wasn't.

Trying to change his focus, he asked, "Want to go for a walk?"

"Sure."

He took Hailey by the hand—a move that surprised him. What was with his urge to touch her?

When she didn't balk, he quit thinking about it and led her to the sidewalk along Tidal Way and to the variety of shops that sold everything from T-shirts to antiques.

They stopped for a while in front of Granny's Fudge Kitchen, looking through the window to watch a guy stir melted chocolate in a huge copper pot that sat over a stove of some kind.

"Thanks for bringing me here," Hailey said. "It's so peaceful and quaint."

"You're welcome. I figured you needed a change of scenery."

"And you didn't?"

Yeah, he did, too. Hospitals always made him edgy. And with Harry going under the knife soon… well, today probably hadn't been easy on either of them.

"I guess we both needed a break." He glanced to the west, watched the sunlight glisten upon the surface of the water, heard a gull cry out as it swooped near the shore. "Whenever I get a chance to escape from the real world, I head for the beach."

"When I want to get away," she said, "I go out to a little fishing hole near my house in Walden."

He found it hard to imagine pretty, fastidious Hailey handling bait or gutting a couple of walleyes. "Do you fish?"

"No. I just take a book, pack a lunch, sit near the shore and read." Her voice held a wistful tone, and her gaze snagged his. "Walden is a great little town. I can't imagine living anywhere else."

That was yet another reason a relationship with a guy born and bred in southern California wouldn't work.

They continued along for a while, glancing at a window display of Christmas ornaments with a small, fake tree boasting a seaside motif, its branches chock-full of shells, starfish and miniature lighthouses that blinked on and off.

They didn't talk much.

Both were lost in their thoughts, Nick supposed. Funny thing was, he kind of enjoyed walking like this, lazy and aimless, looking in store windows. Having Hailey at his side.

Nick had always remained emotionally distant from women in the past, but Hailey was different. His concern for her, of course, was due to her relationship with Harry. And in addition to that, those disclosures they'd shared on that snowy night in Minnesota had given them some kind of bond. Revelations from the past did that sometimes.

But thoughts of that snowbound night triggered another memory. And Nick couldn't shake the desire to make love to Hailey one last time. To feel the heat, the way their bodies had melded. The way they had climaxed together, then held each other throughout the night.

Sex didn't get much better than that.

But a sexual relationship was out of the question, and there was no need to complicate things between him and Hailey any further. So he did his damnedest to shrug off an unwelcome arousal.

He glanced at the woman beside him, noted that she, too, had been quiet. Introspective.

Unable to quell his curiosity, he asked, "What are you thinking about?"

"Nothing," Hailey told him.

But that couldn't have been any further from the truth. At one time she'd fantasized about being part of a real family. About having lots of happy voices in her home. That's why she'd planned to create a family of her own.

Well, now she had one—sort of. That was, of course, assuming a remote, long-distance relationship with Harry was possible.

But did she want one?

Hailey had lived for years believing she didn't need a father. And maybe she still didn't.

But the sorry fact was, Harry was the only grandparent her child would have.

Didn't her baby need a grandpa?

Maybe so, but telling Harry about the baby would make it darn near impossible to keep the secret from Nick.

She stole a glance at the man beside her. Should she tell him? Or keep the news of the baby to herself?

Having struggled with the dilemma for weeks, she was still no closer to an answer.

A childish squeal and laughter rang out ahead, drawing Hailey's attention. A man, woman and child—a family no doubt—rollerbladed along the boardwalk.

"Daddy, watch me," a little girl in pigtails called out. "I didn't fall down for a long time!"

"You're doing great, sweetheart." The man cast a smile at his wife, then took her hand as they skated along.

Hailey touched her tummy, flat now but soon to expand.

That's what she wanted for her baby. Happiness. A normal family life. A mom and dad. A dog and a cat waiting at home.

She glanced at Nick, saw that his eyes were on the skaters, too.

Did she dare broach the subject? Find out how he felt about kids and picket fences? She tucked a fly-away wisp of hair behind her ear, trying to keep the pesky strand in place. "They look like a nice family. Don't you think?"

Nick merely nodded.

Unwilling to give up, she pushed a little further. "Can you ever see yourself doing something like that? You know, taking your son or daughter out to play?"

The question took Nick aback. He again looked at the family, and although it pleased him to see the little girl so happy and to see parents spending quality time with their child, he'd never harbored any dumb idea of having a kid of his own. "Nope. I'm not cut out to be a husband or a father."

"You don't want kids?" she asked, her eyes snagging his and making him feel as if he should have lied.

He opted for the truth. "Kids deserve a lot more than what I could ever give them. Besides, I like my life just the way it is."

Uncomplicated. No one to harp at him and make him feel guilty for not being something he wasn't.

She didn't answer, and he had a feeling he'd disappointed her, although he wasn't sure why.

Nick didn't hold any fantasies about life. His early years had been a nightmare, to say the least. "I wouldn't know what to do with a kid if I had one. Hell, I spent the biggest part of my childhood trying to find places to go, reasons to avoid going home. What do I know about kids or normal families?"

"Parenting should come naturally," she said, her voice soft yet laden with emotion, "although I know it doesn't."

He figured she was thinking of her mom's inability to provide the right kind of home for her as a child. "Not everyone should be a parent. My stepdad's natural inclination was to knock me across the room for the hell of it."

"I suppose parenting, as well as conflict resolution, takes some training, especially if a kid didn't have a good example." She turned, facing him, eyes probing his in a way that reached somewhere deep in his heart. "But you said Harry and Kay had a good marriage, that they showed you what a family was like."

They had, but that didn't mean Nick was going to be any good at it. He might try to emulate his mentor in many ways, but not as a family man. If he tried, he knew he'd fall short of the mark. "I'm not like Harry."

"Well," Hailey said, slowing her steps. "If you don't mind, I'd like to go home."

"Sure. What's the matter?"

"Nothing," she said. "I'm just tired."

Maybe so, but Nick had the feeling he hadn't told her what she wanted to hear. But who could argue with the truth?

Nick wasn't cut out to be a husband or a father. And there was no reason to pretend he was.

Hailey didn't know why Nick's admission hurt the way it had. It's not as though she ever really harbored any kind of belief that the two of them had a future together.

Her life was in Minnesota. And his was in California.

Yet, as senseless as it all was, she felt like crying for no reason at all.

As they climbed from the car and headed toward the elevator that would take them to his loft, he asked, "Are you sure you're okay?"

"Don't worry about me."

She supposed it hurt to know that, should Hailey decide to tell Nick she was pregnant, her baby's father wouldn't want to be a part of their child's life.

Memories of the past, of her own disappointments as a little girl, came back to taunt her. To remind her that her son or daughter would face some of the same pain—all because the father of her baby didn't want to be strapped with a wife and kid.

"You're awfully quiet," he said.

"I'll be just fine."

And she would. Everything would work out. Once she went back home. To Minnesota.

Nick stepped in front of her to unlock the door, then waited as she entered the spacious but cluttered apartment. Before she could slip off her shoes or plop on the sofa, his cell phone rang.

"Granger," he answered. His eyes narrowed, his expression grew serious.

Was it the hospital? Kay? Hailey stood at his side, unable to move.

"I'll be right there."

I'll be right there? Not *we?* Was it a personal call having nothing to do with Harry?

Nick shut off the phone and slipped it back into place on his belt, then turned to her. "I've got to go down to the precinct. It's a big case I've been working on. And even though I asked for time off, my job isn't like—"

She reached for his arm, stroked the sleeve of his worn leather jacket. "You don't have to explain. I understand."

"You do?" he asked.

If Nick were her husband or lover, she might feel different. She might resent having him called away at any time of the day or night. But she had no claims on him. "I know your job places a lot of demands on you."

"Maybe so, but I feel kind of guilty leaving you alone in a strange city on your first day in town."

"Don't give it a second thought. It's not like I'm on vacation." She tossed him a smile, yet felt her eyes grow misty.

For goodness sake. What was wrong with her? It had to be hormones.

"I still hate leaving you alone," he said.

"I don't need to be entertained." She tried to break free of the contradictory swing of emotions that rattled her foundation.

Nick caught her jaw in his hand, his gaze searching her face for something.

Sincerity? Shoot, she understood his line of work better than he realized.

"I know it's not like we have a thing," Nick said. "Well…you know."

His thumb caressed her cheek, sending a flutter of warmth along her skin, making her momentarily wish they did have a thing, whatever that might be.

But thinking like that was crazy. Foolish. And bound to screw things up in her otherwise organized world.

She stepped away, from his touch, his gaze. His scent. There was no point in thinking about the attraction between them. Or at least the star-crossed attraction she felt for a man who would turn her life upside down.

A relationship with Nick Granger would crash and burn.

"Go on," she said, waving him off. "I'll watch television. Or take a nap. Don't worry about me."

For a moment she thought he might brush his lips across hers, give her a kiss before leaving. But he cleared his throat and said goodbye.

"Take care of yourself." She followed him to the door with a pasted-on smile, yet struggled with another senseless urge to cry—for no reason at all.

It was just a case of the weepies, she decided, brought on by hormones.

Why else would she feel so sad and alone?

It's not as if she didn't know how to take care of herself. She'd been on her own for ages.

Damn those hormones. She blinked back the moisture in her eyes, trying hard to hide the emotion from Nick.

And she did.

But when the door closed behind him, the tears slid down her cheeks.

For no reason at all.

Chapter Eight

By six o'clock that evening, Hailey had grown tired of looking at Nick's clutter, even with a big-screen television and surround sound to distract her.

She started by straightening the magazines on the glass-top coffee table, which, she realized, would look a lot nicer without water rings, smudges and a film of dust. So, she went to the kitchen to find something to wipe down the tabletop, only to be sidetracked by a sinkful of dirty dishes. There weren't *that* many, but they'd sat in the kitchen until the food had dried like speckles of colorful concrete.

While two plates, a bowl, three glasses and some odd pieces of flatware soaked in hot, soapy water, she wiped down the counters, gathering more dust than crumbs. And, before she knew it, she was elbow deep in a spring cleaning that should have taken place last year, or the one before that.

She didn't know what compelled her to open the refrigerator—curiosity, probably—but she clicked her tongue when she studied the stark contents.

A quart of milk. A take-out container from a Chinese restaurant. An opened case of Mexican beer with a couple of bottles missing. A jar of jalapeño peppers. Mustard and ketchup. Hot sauce. And a partial cube of butter that had, over time, become a refrigerator odor eater.

No bread, no fruit. No cheese. What did this guy eat when he wanted a snack?

She peeked into the white carton decorated with a red Oriental dragon and scrunched her nose at the dried, shriveled contents. God only knew what it had once been. Maybe something with noodles, but definitely not edible. She tossed the entire container into the trash can.

Better check the date on the jug of milk, she told herself. November 2. Yuck. You'd think an observant detective would pay attention to things like best-when-used-by dates.

Hailey went to the sink and, holding her breath, poured out the milk, watching big white clumps that looked like cottage cheese plop into the drain. Thank goodness her earlier bout of morning sickness had passed.

Sheesh. What a mess.

Hailey liked things tidy, liked a home to be cozy and warm, something Nick didn't seem to care about.

It wasn't as though his place was uninhabitable. But obviously he spent very little time here.

She recalled the words she'd told the students who frequented the school library, whenever they squabbled with each other and came to her for advice. Just because someone isn't like you, doesn't mean they're not special in their own way.

It might be best if she put her own philosophy to work in this case. Hailey and Nick wanted different things out of life, and they didn't appear to have anything in common.

Except a baby.

She blew out a ragged sigh. She certainly couldn't build her hopes on a child drawing them together.

Nick didn't want kids, a wife, a family.

She stooped to open the cupboard under the sink and found cleaning supplies in a nifty blue organizer similar to the one she used to tote along with her when she scrubbed at home.

Inside the carryall she found cleanser, springtime-scented bleach, lemon oil for the furniture and window spray.

Why on earth would Nick purchase this stuff if he had no intention of using it?

Tucked behind the can of cleanser, she found a pair of rubber gloves. Pink. Size small.

Jealousy, or something darn near like it, poked at her chest. Who was the woman who'd purchased this?

She told herself that whoever had placed the items under the sink—be it a lover or a hired cleaning lady—hadn't used them in quite some time. And even if they'd been used yesterday, it didn't matter. Hailey Conway had no claims on Nick Granger. And she didn't want any.

She had high expectations for a marriage, for a home. Why, she and Nick would probably go ten rounds before any vows could be spoken.

Vows?

For goodness sake, that obtrusive thought must have been triggered by domestic drudgery. What was wrong with her? Hailey needed to focus on reality, not whimsy.

So she dug in and got busy, making the detective's place sparkle and shine.

She scanned the once stale and dusty loft apartment, inhaling the clean, lemony scent, and hoped she hadn't overstepped her boundaries, hoped that she hadn't set herself up for a confrontation. Nick might not appreciate her cleaning his house. In fact, he might consider her efforts intrusive.

Well, it was too late now. She'd just have to face the consequences of his irritation when he got home.

What had he said?

I like my life the way it is.

Well, she liked the life she'd created for herself, too.

Except it would be nice to have a husband, a helpmate. A father for her baby.

Again the past cropped up on her, taunting her with memories of growing up without a dad, without a mom, too, she supposed. But her baby's life would be different. She'd see to that.

Hailey would be the best single mother in the whole world. And someday, God willing, she'd find her baby a wonderful stepfather, a man who was willing to take his family on a Saturday-afternoon picnic, who'd build a swing set and climbing structure in the backyard. A loving, happy man who would sit with Hailey in the front row and cheer when the curtain lifted during the Walden Elementary School spring program.

Who needed Nick Granger?

Not Hailey.

And not her baby.

Nick parked the Jeep in his allotted space, then proceeded to the elevator, tired but relieved. They'd finally caught up with Joey Kramer—that no-good piece of crap—and gotten a confession.

The bastard known as the Downtown Rapist would spend the rest of his life behind bars, thanks to the department's careful handling of the case. Search warrants had been obtained and served appropriately, Miranda rights had been read. The investigation and apprehension had been textbook perfect. And the D.A.'s office was as pleased as the guys on the force.

Joey Kramer would be doing serious time.

Normally Nick came home after an arrest like Kramer's feeling proud as hell and pumped, the adrenaline flowing in a way that made sleep tough.

And he felt like that now, but the buzz from the

interrogation and subsequent confession was diluted with guilt for leaving Hailey alone.

He half expected to enter the house and find her pacing the floor—like Carla had done on numerous occasions. His old lover was actually a great lady, but when she got mad at Nick, she morphed into a broom-riding nag.

Braced for the worst, but trying to be considerate and quiet in case Hailey was asleep, Nick let himself in.

The room was dark, lit only by the city lights shining through the living room window. But the scent of lemon and pine accosted him, letting him know that instead of spending time watching television, Hailey had scrubbed and cleaned.

And, no doubt, gotten worked up in the process.

Damn. Would he have to listen to her gripe about the way he put toilet paper on the spindle? Or have her rag on him about the grungy shower curtain that suited him just fine?

Not tonight, he supposed. Hailey was as quiet as a country mouse. He made his way through the room, until he spotted her asleep on the sofa. Her hair spread out on a pillow she'd taken from the bed, her eyes closed softly, her mouth slightly parted.

She wore an oversize T-shirt—nothing special, and certainly not silk or satin—but for some damn reason she looked as sexy as hell.

He had the urge to wake her, take her to his bed, to taste her, love her. But he couldn't—wouldn't—

do that, although a growing arousal argued that his conscience had better damn well reconsider.

But other than a temporary affair, he had nothing to offer Hailey. And besides, wasn't there something morally wrong about sleeping with his friend's daughter? Sleeping with her more than once, anyway. Hell, even a rebel had his principles.

Go take a shower, his conscience suggested. *Stop watching her like a perverted Peeping Tom.*

But Nick's feet wouldn't move.

Maybe it would be okay to wake her, just so she could fall back asleep in his bed. Where she belonged.

Hadn't they agreed that the sofa was supposed to be his while she stayed here?

Hey, his conscience said, *don't use that flimsy excuse as a reason to wake her.*

But he shook off the thought, reached out and touched Hailey's arm, jostling her softly. "Hey."

She opened her eyes, then stretched like a cat napping in the sun and sent him a sleepy-eyed smile.

Nick might have made up his mind to keep his hands to himself, but somebody should have told his arms. And his libido. He had an overwhelming urge to brush a kiss against her lips. To waken that fiery passion that bubbled just under her surface, the passion he knew burned hot.

"Sorry to wake you," he lied. "I thought you might want to go to bed."

Her mouth opened, and her eyes widened.

"I meant to sleep," he corrected. Yet he wasn't

thinking about sleep. He was thinking about sliding his hands under the hem of her nightshirt, of running his fingers along her skin, seeking out her breasts and making her nipples harden.

He raked a hand through his hair instead.

"What time is it?" she asked.

"About midnight."

She sat up and looked around the room. "It feels like morning."

"I figured you might clobber me if I carried you to bed." He nodded toward the foot of the couch, where the spare blanket had bunched up at her bare feet. "I'm supposed to take the sofa."

"I don't mind." She stifled a yawn, then got up and padded toward the kitchen. The shirt she wore barely covered a pair of gray flannel shorts, revealing shapely legs. Legs that had once wrapped around him.

He watched as she reached into the cupboard and took out a glass.

"I've got beer in the fridge," he said. "Milk, too, I think."

"No, thanks. And the milk is gone." She turned on the spigot and filled her glass with water. "By the way, you need to stock your cupboards better. I ate your last can of tuna."

Feeling like a lousy host, he said, "I...uh...eat out a lot. I figured we'd..."

"It's okay," she said. "I ate some of the saltines, too. If you pick up some plastic containers at the store, your crackers will keep longer."

A can of tuna fish and stale crackers. That was a hell of a meal. He'd hightailed it out of here so fast he hadn't thought about feeding her. And she was right. He didn't stock much of anything in his house, finding it easier to pick up fast food. "When I got that call from my partner, I just…I'm sorry, Hailey."

"I'm a big girl." She drank the water, then replaced the glass in the sink.

"How about I make it up to you by taking you out to breakfast in the morning?"

"Don't worry about it." She padded back to the sofa and plopped down.

"And I'll take you someplace tomorrow. Old Town, maybe. Or Balboa Park."

"It's not a problem, Detective. I kept busy."

She'd kept busy, all right, cleaning up his apartment, and building up a ton of resentment. He braced himself for a broom-flying attack.

But she didn't say anything, didn't complain. Which, he decided, was worse. Because instead of feeling defensive, he felt something else. Guilt, maybe, although he wasn't entirely sure why. This was his life. His place. Which had been arguments he'd shot at Carla whenever she tried to make him into something he wasn't.

"Want to watch television?" she asked. "I'm not sure if I can go back to sleep."

Nick figured he was in for a long night, too. "Why not?"

She picked up the remote and clicked until she found a chick flick already in progress. But before he could suggest something else, something with some action, she said, "I love this movie. And Meg Ryan is my favorite actress."

Oh, no. Not a romantic comedy. Not tonight. He could sure use a little shoot 'em up right now. A few explosions. Some bones breaking, Steven Segal style.

He started to object, but with Hailey at his side, looking as sweet and cuddly as Meg Ryan ever did, he squirmed in his seat instead.

"Have you ever seen *When Harry Met Sally?*" she asked.

"Nope." But he liked Billy Crystal, so maybe there'd be a few laughs. Something to take his mind off the pretty brunette sitting next to him, with her bare legs tucked under her.

Surprisingly, the movie drew his interest. And when Meg's character discussed women faking orgasms while sitting across the table from Billy's character in a crowded restaurant, Nick couldn't help but chuckle, especially when Meg went into great detail while showing Billy how easily it was done.

Nick shot a glance at Hailey, caught her stealing a look at him. Had she ever faked an orgasm?

Not with him, of course. The climaxes she'd had with him had been real. Earth-shattering. The kind to make a guy want to pummel his chest, Tarzan-style.

"She's right, you know." Hailey grinned.

Breaking his vow not to bring up that night, not to stir memories of hot sex on a cold night, Nick said, "You weren't faking with me."

She sort of chuckled in that feminine way that suggested men didn't know squat about women, which was true, he supposed. But she hadn't faked anything with him. No way. No woman was that good an actress. But it struck a blow to his ego, making his male pride falter just a tad.

Hailey merely grinned, although she wasn't sure why. He was right. That night in Minnesota had been good. Darn good. Maybe she didn't want him to know how much of an effect he'd had on her. He still had.

She turned in her seat, knees drawn up in a protective posture, and she tossed him a crooked smile, taunting him without words.

"You didn't fake anything," he said.

Maybe it was the all-knowing tone of his voice, or the glimmer of doubt she spotted in his eye. Either way, it made her want to tease about a subject they had no business broaching. "I guess you'll never know for sure."

"Maybe not," he said. "But don't even go there, honey. Or I'll make you eat your words."

For a moment, his threat—or was it a promise?—hung in the air, waiting for action. Or reaction. The sexual energy that had been so strong in Minnesota came back full force.

Hailey didn't dare move, didn't dare open the door they'd both closed on the intimacy they'd shared. Yet her body screamed out in frustration, like a child throwing a temper tantrum.

She wanted to lean forward. Touch him. Place her

mouth on his. Taste the spearmint flavor of the breath mints he favored.

And when she saw the passion in his gaze, saw the struggle he fought, she turned toward the television. Tried to focus on the movie. But her efforts to sidetrack the subject failed.

Her mind wanted only one thing. To feel Nick Granger's hands on her again. To kiss him as though there were no secrets between them, no reason on God's green earth why they shouldn't enter a full-blown love affair.

"I didn't fake anything," she admitted. "It was pretty good, as far as sex goes."

"It was better than good," he muttered. "But I think we both know better than to get involved like that again."

Yes, she supposed that was true. But something deep inside, something decidedly female and wistful, wanted more. Wanted something that couldn't possibly be good for her.

She unwrapped her legs from under her and stood, tugging at the boxer-style shorts she wore. Then she made her way to the window, to the starry display of city lights.

"You agree, don't you?" Nick followed her to the window, stood behind her, close enough for her to savor his musky scent, to catch a whiff of spearmint. "That a repeat of that night isn't going to do either of us a bit of good."

He placed a hand on her shoulder, as though wanting to turn her around, to make her face him, to face what had happened in Minnesota.

But how could she? How could she admit to having a weakness when it came to Nick Granger? Admit that she had big plans for her future, plans that didn't include a brief affair with a man she had no business pursuing, a man who weakened her knees and turned her inside out.

Wouldn't the intimacy of making love again only further complicate things?

Hadn't he said as much?

A repeat of that night isn't going to do either of us any good.

Hailey turned, her eyes landing on his. "I've always thought a sexual relationship should be built upon more than a healthy libido."

A slow grin tugged at his lips. "That's the woman in you speaking. A guy doesn't mind having a great sexual relationship. But women start wanting more."

"Then, there you have it." She tried to return his smile. "We couldn't have anything more than great sex."

"You're right."

This was one time Hailey wished she wasn't right, wished that Nick could convince her to share his bed, to consider sharing more than that. Their baby, maybe.

He placed a kiss upon her cheek in a brotherly manner.

But the heat that pooled in her belly was anything

but a sisterly response. How could a man who was so wrong for her stir such desire?

There was more to a relationship than sex. More to a home than a man and woman living under one roof. There was teamwork. And love.

But that wasn't something she wanted to talk to Nick about. Not tonight.

"I think I'll turn in," she said.

"Sure."

They stood there like that for a while, as though both struggling with common sense and desire.

Then Hailey tossed him a lighthearted smile, one she hoped masked the heavy-duty thoughts that warred inside her brain. "Good night."

Nick stepped aside. "Sleep tight."

Fat chance of that, she thought, as she slipped behind the screen that provided very little privacy.

Sleep would be a long time coming tonight.

And maybe for several nights to follow.

Chapter Nine

Nick slept like crap.

But that didn't surprise him. He'd struggled with his conscience and his sex drive until dawn. Memories of his and Hailey's lovemaking had driven him wild with need. He'd relived each touch, each kiss, each thrust until he thought he'd go nuts.

Try as he might, he couldn't forget the night he and Hailey had broken the rules. And knowing that she lay within reach hadn't helped cool his heels or his arousal.

Still, he'd managed to stay on the sofa, which ought to count for something. He wondered whether God—or whoever the Almighty put in charge of passing out the gold stars in Heaven—had noticed that the one-time rebel had behaved himself.

Nick had never been a saint—far from it. So he figured a few good moves on his part, like getting criminals off the street, or, in this case, keeping his hands off Harry Logan's daughter, might score a few points for a guy who'd once been headed straight to hell. Lord knew he had a lot of making up to do.

He finally dozed off around four, only to be awakened by something that sounded a lot like someone heaving. Or maybe it was a garbage truck rumbling by.

Squinting at the sunlight pouring in the window, he glanced at the clock: 9:14. Time to get up, he supposed. But another gut-wrenching heave drew his attention.

What the heck? Was Hailey sick?

He knocked on the bathroom door. "Are you okay?"

"I'm," she managed to say between gags, "f-f...fine."

She didn't sound fine. Shoot, she hadn't eaten much last night. Tuna and saltines, she'd said. Maybe the canned fish had gone bad.

Where the hell had that tuna come from? Since he didn't particularly like the stuff, and Carla had tried to make some godawful casseroles, he guessed that she'd bought it. But hell, it was possible the darn can had been in the pantry when he moved in.

Maybe the lid had bulged, and Hailey hadn't noticed. And if she ate it...

She heaved again.

Oh, for cripe's sake. What was wrong with her? Botulism? Salmonella? Or just a case of stomach flu?

"Can I get you something?" he asked.

"No."

A few minutes later the toilet flushed, and he waited for her to come out. It seemed like forever, but when she finally stepped through the door, her eyes were red and watery, and she was ghostly pale. "Are you sure you're okay?"

"Don't worry about me," she reiterated.

As she made her way toward the bed like a drunken sailor on his first shore leave in months, her steps faltered, and she tried to steady herself by placing a hand on the wall.

Nick stepped forward, which was a darn good thing, because her legs went out from under her, and he managed to catch her just in time.

God, was he in trouble now. Not only had he slept with Harry's daughter while in Minnesota, but he'd brought her to California only to make her sick.

He placed her on the bed and watched her eyelids flutter. She appeared to have fainted.

He was supposed to be trained to handle this kind of stuff. But he stood there, unmoving, like a stone-cold statue of some dead hero in the park.

He watched Hailey come to, her face pale, her eyes slowly opening. She seemed to focus, to recognize him, he supposed. But she looked miserable. As much as he was tempted to call 911 and get some backup, he braced himself to wait it out. To figure out what he was up against.

"I'm sorry," she said.

She was sorry? "For what?"

"For being a bother, I guess." She closed her eyes and blew out a weak sigh.

"You're not a bother. But I'm going to call a doctor. Maybe take you to the E.R. and have someone look you over."

Hopefully, Nick's friend, Luke Wynter, was on call. Once a delinquent like Nick, Luke had straightened out his life, too, thanks to Harry. The E.R. resident was a whiz when it came to bullet holes, knife wounds and broken bones. An upset stomach should be a piece of cake.

"I don't need a doctor." Hailey slowly sat up in bed, then placed a hand on her forehead and grimaced. "I'm just a little light-headed from not eating much yesterday."

Again Nick felt like a jerk. Okay, so he hadn't been responsible for poisoning Harry's daughter. But he'd damn near starved her to death—if he could believe what she said about her illness being no big deal.

"Are you sure you're only woozy from not eating?" he asked.

"I'm sure."

He furrowed his brow. "Then why did you throw up?"

"Too much bile in my tummy, I guess." She offered him a puny smile and a shrug.

"Then I better feed you. There's a great diner just a block or two away. How about we go have some breakfast?'' He was thinking something hearty, like steak and eggs. Biscuits and gravy. Something that would fill her up and keep her going until the next meal.

"Getting some breakfast is probably a good idea, but right now I could sure use a piece of toast. Or maybe some crackers."

"How about those stale saltines?" he asked, trying to make light of his meager food supply.

"I'll take whatever you've got." She blew out a weak sigh. "And could you hurry?"

Nick left Hailey on the bed and went in search of the crackers, although he thought it might be better to call in the paramedics. Hell, he'd seen enough blood and guts during a routine homicide investigation to handle this kind of thing with ease. But for some reason, this was different. This was Hailey. His mentor's daughter. A woman who'd been placed in his care.

When he entered the kitchen, he realized she'd done more than wash the dishes and wipe down the counters. Sunlight glistened through the window, and he caught his reflection in the chrome on the stove, the oven, too. Shoot, even Carla hadn't cleaned the kitchen this thoroughly.

He opened the cupboard that served as a pantry, and although there wasn't much of anything there, each can was stacked neatly. Just as organized as her cupboards back home.

Was Hailey nesting in his house? Moving in, like Carla had done?

Nick found the thought both disturbing and comforting, which was too weird to contemplate. He sure as hell didn't need another woman around on a day-to-day basis, pointing out his flaws. Reminding him why he wasn't husband material.

He snatched the box of saltines from the cupboard, wondering if stale crackers would do her any good, but he took them to her, anyway.

"Thanks." She set the whole box in her lap while she dug inside, then popped a cracker in her mouth. The color had returned to her cheeks. And she appeared to have recovered.

He watched as she took another cracker from the pack. Hell, he couldn't let her fill up on those damn things. "I'll take a quick shower, then we're going to eat a real meal."

"That sounds good to me." She smiled at him, and a rush of heat slammed into his gut. She looked damn good sitting cross-legged on his bed, her hair tousled from sleep.

He grumbled under his breath. What was wrong with him? The poor woman had been sick, passed out from lack of food, and here he was, salivating over the sight of her sitting amidst rumpled sheets.

Maybe he just needed to get laid. Needed a warm, willing woman—not Hailey, mind you—but another woman who would get his mind off sex and off Harry's daughter. Only trouble was, he couldn't conjure an image that appealed to him. Other than Hailey. The way she'd looked that night in the candlelit bedroom. Hell, even the way she looked right now.

There she sat, eating crackers in his bed. Probably scattering crumbs all over the sheets.

And he didn't mind a bit.

Trying to get his horny thoughts back on track, back on the shower he'd intended to take, Nick said, "I'll only be a minute. Then it's your turn."

She merely popped another cracker in her mouth and nodded, so he disappeared behind the bathroom door and turned the tap on full blast.

While he waited for the water to heat, he scanned the small room. She'd left her mark here, too. The sink had been scrubbed, the mirror shined. And two blue towels—in almost new condition—hung neatly on the rack. Hell, even the shower curtain didn't appear grungy. How'd she do that?

Better not ask. Not if he didn't want to get an earful of how sloppy he was.

Nick slipped off his shirt and sweatpants, then climbed into the shower, relished the spray of hot water that splashed on his back. And when he'd finished, he snatched one of the towels she'd hung on the rack and dried off.

Now for a quick shave. He searched the counter where he usually kept his razor and found it bare, other than a new bar of soap sitting on a small glass bowl she'd gotten from the kitchen.

Where the heck had she hidden his shaving gear? He didn't have to look too hard. She'd stashed it in the mirrored medicine chest. Right where it belonged, he supposed, but he'd always kept things out in the open. Where he could easily find them.

He glanced in the mirror, now fogged by steam, and swiped his hand across the glass to clear a spot to see. Intent on getting Hailey to the diner to feed her, he tried to hurry, without cutting himself. And when he'd finished, he dried his face with the damp towel, saving the one still hanging on the rack for her.

Then he slapped on a dab of aftershave and looked in the mirror. Not bad.

And no blood.

He draped the used towel over the rack so it could dry, then went out to tell Hailey the bathroom was all hers.

Hailey waited for her turn to shower, hoping that this nasty bout of morning sickness had passed. Gosh, she'd even fainted.

How long would these pregnancy symptoms last? And, more important, how long could she keep her condition a secret from Nick?

Thank goodness he'd bought her story about being light-headed from lack of food. Although, she really *was* dying to get something in her tummy. Something that would stay put.

"It's all yours," he said, when he came out of the bathroom.

"Thanks. I'll make it quick." She went to the closet, where she'd hung the few things she'd packed, and pulled out a pair of slacks and a sweater to wear for the day. But before she could enter the bathroom, the phone rang. It might not be any of her business, but she paused long enough to hear Nick say, "How's he doing this morning?"

The call was about Harry. Her father.

And as much as she wanted a shower and a meal, she waited to hear the news.

"Good," Nick said. "When are they going to do it?"

Hailey wasn't able to decipher much from Nick's side of the conversation, only enough to know the surgery had been scheduled.

"I'm glad your sons are with you. Tell them I said hello."

When he hung up, he told her, "They're going to do the bypass tomorrow morning."

She nodded. "That's good, I guess."

"Yeah," was all he said.

Worry was etched on his brow, and she sympathized. Harry was like a dad to him. Losing his friend and mentor would hurt. It would hurt her, too, although she'd always thought she'd lost her father years ago.

But she'd been given a second chance at a relationship with Harry. If she wanted it. And if he lived through the surgery. Worry niggled at her, as well as guilt. God wouldn't be so cruel as to open the door for a reunion, a reconciliation, then slam it shut. Would He?

Harry would live. He had to.

"In the past few years bypass surgery has become routine, hasn't it?" That's what Hailey had heard, anyway, and she hoped her words would ease Nick's mind. Ease her own, too, she supposed.

"Harry's heart was damaged when he suffered the heart attack. And he has some other complications, too. That's what made them keep him in the hospital and put off the surgery until now."

Without a thought, other than to offer support, Hailey strode toward the rugged detective and gave him a hug. In spite of her intention to offer friendship and compassion, his clean, musky scent enveloped her, offering her something in return. Something she instinctively wanted to hold on to.

Nick slid his hand along her back in a comforting gesture. An appreciative gesture. Or was it more like a lover's caress?

He held her close, as though never wanting to let her go. As though needing her comfort, her presence. Which, she supposed, was understandable.

Harry was all Nick had. All she had, too. Except for the baby.

Again she pondered telling Nick she was pregnant, but held her tongue. The time wasn't right. But would the time ever be right to tell a man who didn't want children that he was about to become a father?

"Well," Hailey said, wanting to break the connection before the embrace turned into something more. Something intimate. And revealing. "I'd better get into the shower."

When he released her and stepped away, she went into the bathroom, closed the door and turned the lock.

Standing in the small room, she tried to regroup. She had to get her scattered emotions under control. There was a lot going on in her life right now. The stuff with her father, his surgery. The baby. The darn hormones that were wreaking havoc on her body.

She glanced at the mirror, saw the smudge where a hand had wiped the glass. Then she spotted the blue towel Nick had used to dry off and then draped haphazardly on the rack. She'd meant for it to be displayed, not used.

She blew out a sigh. Even the remaining towel hung skewed and uneven. She clicked her tongue and straightened them both, then reached into the cupboard under the sink for another towel.

A woman would have her hands full trying to keep that man's house clean, to make his house a home.

And Hailey wasn't up to the task.

Nick took Hailey to Auntie Em's, a mom-and-pop-style diner that offered down-home food and sported a *Wizard of Oz* decor.

"I don't normally like cutesy restaurants with a theme," Nick said, "but this is close to my building and the food is good."

"I think it's darling." Hailey scanned the farmhouse-type setting, the wooden tables with red-and-white-checkered tablecloths, each one boasting a salt and pepper shaker made of Depression-era glass and a Mason jar full of fresh daisies in the center.

A mural on one wall depicted Dorothy and her friends walking along the yellow-brick road with the

Emerald City in the distance. Instead of birds, several winged monkeys flew in a cloudy sky.

The waitresses all wore blue gingham dresses with white cotton aprons and tennis shoes covered in sparkling red stones that looked like rubies. Even the busboy, a tall, lanky teenager, was costumed as a farmhand in denim overalls with a red kerchief in the rear pocket.

The hostess, a matronly woman wearing a name tag saying Auntie Em, seated them at a table for two near the window that allowed them a view of the busy street. "Can I get you some coffee?"

"Yeah," Nick said. "Black."

"I'll have tea," Hailey said.

The woman brought their drinks, then left them alone with an old-fashioned menu tucked in a plastic cover, resembling those used in the thirties and forties.

Hailey smiled at the names of the daily breakfast specials: the Scarecrow Scramble, Toto's Towering Hotcakes, the Wizard's Waffle and Auntie Em's Ham and Egg Surprise.

"They make great homemade biscuits and gravy," Nick said. "Now that's a meal that will stick with you all day long."

Ugh. Even the thought of bacon or sausage drippings brought back a rush of nausea. "No, thanks. I can imagine that gravy sticking to my arteries instead of my ribs."

"Their sausage is great, too," Nick added, obviously wanting to fill her up. And out.

But again his suggestions only made her stomach act up. "I think I'll have the Kansas Twister."

"What's that?" He scanned the menu then scrunched his nose. "A fruit smoothie? That isn't going to stay with you very long."

It would probably stay with her longer than the sausage or gravy would, she suspected. "I like eating healthy. But I am hungry, so maybe I'll have a home-made biscuit, too."

Nick made a grunt-like sound, one she suspected men had been making since the cave-dwelling days. But he didn't argue.

The strawberry-banana-yogurt drink hit the spot, and Hailey drank every last drop. Funny thing about this morning sickness. It seemed to come and go at will. It sure didn't act like the intestinal flu, even though it felt the same when it struck with a vengeance.

When the waitress handed Nick the check and he paid the bill at the front counter, Hailey assumed they'd go home. Or head to the hospital to see Harry.

Nick opened the restaurant door for her. "Let's get my car and go to Balboa Park."

She paused in the doorway. "You don't need to feel guilty about going to work and doing your job."

"I'm not feeling guilty," he said, although she suspected he was, at least a bit. "I don't have to go to work today. And I don't feel like sitting at home and watching TV."

She brushed a strand of hair behind her ear. "You still don't need to entertain me."

"You might not come back to San Diego for a long time." He took her arm and ushered her down the street. "Besides, I think you could use some fresh air."

"Maybe so," she said, walking alongside him as they headed back to the underground parking garage where he'd left his Jeep Wrangler.

Ten minutes later they arrived at Balboa Park, a cultural center that bordered the San Diego Zoo and provided more than a thousand acres of lush gardens and museums.

Struck with a feeling of déjà vu, Hailey realized she'd been here before. A long time ago.

As they climbed from the Jeep, she spotted small train tracks and a choo-choo that offered rides for children. And next to the ticket booth sat an old-fashioned carousel. The memory, bright and clear, came flooding back. Harry had brought her here when she was five.

She'd ridden that merry-go-round. And later that afternoon he'd bought her a souvenir, a little carousel pony that she'd once cherished. A figurine that now rested in a dark box, under her bed and out of sight.

Her steps must have slowed, because Nick asked, "What's the matter?"

"Nothing." And everything.

Nick took her hand, gave it a squeeze. "Are you sick again?"

"No, I'm okay." She flashed him a smile, tried to hide the emotion swirling in her chest. But her heart constricted, and a tear slipped down her face.

"The heck you are." Nick brushed his thumb across her cheek, wiping the telltale sign from her face. His gesture softened her heart and her resolve to keep her memories locked away.

"It's just that I've been here before." She pointed to the merry-go-round. "With Harry."

He nodded as though he understood. And maybe he did. "Want to walk closer?"

"Yes, I'd like that." She wasn't sure whether either of them had actually made the first move, but her hand slipped easily into his.

As they neared the carousel, the military-band-style music grew louder, luring Hailey like a fascinated child to a menagerie of animals and ponies, each one unique and colorful. And like the little girl she once had been, she longed to buy a ticket and climb on the prettiest pony. To reach for the brass ring.

Years ago she'd held Harry's hand as they walked toward the carousel. Now she held Nick's.

As they neared the ticket booth, excitement niggled at her, and she squeezed his hand. "I'd like to ride."

"The carousel?" He chuckled. "Really?"

"Do you mind?"

"Not at all. I'll buy you a ticket."

"Get us both one. I want you to ride with me."

The goofy look he gave her was priceless.

Was she crazy? Nick wasn't going to get on a kiddie ride. But as Hailey looked at him with those big blue eyes, his macho resolve turned to mush. "How about if I stand next to you?"

She flashed him a smile that lit her face, just like any of the other kids clamoring for a ride on the antique ponies. And just like some of the doting dads and grandpas, he followed her onto the carousel.

She chose a white horse that had an ornate red saddle trimmed in blue and yellow, then shot him a silly smile that touched his heart in a sappy way. Made him feel things he'd never felt. A part of him wanted to make a mad dash and escape, another wanted him to hang on to the moment.

"I'm going to try and get the brass ring," she said, eyes glowing and showing him a side of her he'd never seen.

People, mostly kids and parents, began to fill the carousel, taking their places on giraffes, lions and bears, but Nick felt strangely alone. Just him and Hailey, in a surreal world of their own.

And when she flashed him another of those Meg Ryan smiles, he couldn't help himself. He placed a hand on the back of her neck, under the silky tresses of hair, and pulled her toward him for a kiss.

Her mouth opened, maybe initially in surprise, but she reached for his cheek, drew him near, allowing a kiss he shouldn't have instigated. A kiss that shouldn't taste as sweet as it did. A kiss that nearly knocked him to his knees.

Fortunately, the damn carousel began to move, and the soul-stirring kiss ended as soon as it began.

He thought about apologizing but quickly reconsidered. Hell, what was he sorry for? Feeling attracted to a pretty woman? Liking the way she felt in his arms, the way he felt when he kissed her? Heck, he was only human.

As the pony moved up and down and the carousel moved round and round, Hailey tried to grab the brass ring, coming close once but missing.

On the second time around, someone else had nabbed it before she got a chance. And he noticed a flash of disappointment cross her face.

The rest of the ride was unremarkable, although Nick sensed a sadness in Hailey, as though snagging that brass ring meant a lot more to her than it should have. As though it symbolized something more than a child's game.

A grand prize in the game of life, maybe.

Funny thing, but Nick knew how she felt.

The brass ring had always seemed just out of his reach, too.

Chapter Ten

Even with a fly-by-the-seat-of-his-pants attitude, Nick managed to take Hailey to many of the touristy spots in San Diego, packing it all into one trip, since he wasn't sure how much longer she would be in town.

He expected that giving her a tour of the city would be a wasted, pain-in-the-butt day, yet it wasn't. And the truth was he enjoyed seeing San Diego through Hailey's eyes. He enjoyed being with her, too. She'd relaxed around him, and they'd grown easy together, sharing a camaraderie, it seemed.

As the sun slid low in the afternoon sky, they strolled through Old Town, peeking in some shop windows, wandering inside other stores.

Nick slipped an arm around her, and he wasn't

sure why. He'd never been the touchy/feely type, not in public, anyway. But the move had been completely unplanned on his part—subconscious, actually. And for some reason, with Hailey at his side, it felt right.

She didn't tense or pull away, which told him that she'd accepted the change in their relationship, whatever it was. Maybe the lazy day they'd spent together had caused them to let down their guards. To become friends.

Or was it more than that?

He didn't want to even go there. Not now. It was better just to enjoy her company—while it lasted.

Up ahead, mariachis played for the people who ate at Don Pablo's, a quaint, thatched-roof restaurant that provided patio dining around a stone-crafted fountain. Bright-red bougainvilleas in big clay pots graced the perimeter, giving diners who sat at wrought-iron tables an aura of Old Mexico.

The scent of spicy beef fajitas sizzling in a cast-iron skillet on a nearby table mingled with the breeze that blew in from the sea.

"Want to sit for a while?" Nick asked. "Maybe have some chips and guacamole?"

"Sure." She offered him a bright-eyed smile. "I'd love to listen to the music."

They chose a table near the rustic stone fountain, and before they knew it, a basket of warm tortilla chips as well as a bowl of salsa fresca sat before them.

"Can I get you a drink?" a waitress in a white peasant blouse and a colorful skirt asked.

"The margaritas are the best in town," Nick told Hailey. "You ought to try one."

She reached for a chip and slowly shook her head. "No, thanks. I'd better pass on the alcohol."

"Why?" Nick asked, although he assumed it was because of her earlier stomach problems.

She seemed to ponder the question—or maybe just her response—then flashed him a dimpled grin. "Let's just say I'd like to keep my wits about me."

So she'd felt it, too. The attraction. Yet he suspected there was more going on than that. He'd felt it each time she'd taken his hand, each time she'd touched his arm or tugged at the sleeve of his shirt and pointed at something of interest.

And like a sap, he'd been happy to look, to smile, to laugh.

They'd grown familiar with each other today. Comfortable. And it felt good.

He couldn't help but wonder if a repeat of that passionate, snowbound night was in the cards. The rebel in him hoped so. And for the life of him, he couldn't seem to come up with a reason why making love one more time would be so bad. He slid her a crooked smile. "Afraid a little alcohol will cause you to lose your head around me?"

"It happened before."

Yeah. They'd both lost their heads that housebound evening in Minnesota. And he figured Hailey, too, was contemplating not only the past, but the very near future.

Still, this was the closest they'd actually come to broaching the subject they'd both been avoiding. They'd merely tiptoed around it last night, when they'd talked about women and orgasms—real and fake. But this was the first time either of them had hinted at the temptation of sleeping together again. Of turning a one-night stand into two nights. Maybe three.

The magnitude of anything more with Hailey made Nick squirm in his seat, so he decided to change the subject—at least until they got home.

"I'll have a Mexican beer," he told the waitress.

Hailey ordered a soda.

"And could you bring us a bowl of guacamole?"

"Sure," the dark-haired woman said. "Would you like anything else?"

"How about something to eat?" he asked Hailey. "Pablo makes a great fish taco."

"That sounds good to me." She leaned toward the sound of the mariachis, her face lighting up as she watched the trio of men playing guitars and singing words in Spanish.

Nick understood the language well enough to know the Latino musicians sang a romantic ballad, and even that didn't put a damper on his mood.

Ten minutes later the waitress brought them a bowl of guacamole and two plates laden with beans, rice and tacos.

Nick watched as Hailey took another chip and

scooped at the melted cheese atop the beans and popped it into her mouth. Apparently her nervous stomach had abated since this morning, because she soon began to chow down as if she hadn't had a meal in days.

She glanced up from her plate, a smile gracing her lips. "You were right. This fish taco is delicious."

When she'd finished her meal, every last bite, she licked at a dribble of something or other from her lips.

The sensuous movement of her tongue brought on a rush of heated memories and new desires.

Nick wasn't sure how Hailey would feel about making love for old-times' sake. But he'd be hard-pressed not to suggest it. Tonight. When they got home.

That evening, in Nick's loft apartment, Hailey stood before the window that looked over the city. A million tiny lights sparkled, proving that life went on after dark. And it would go on for her, too.

Something happened today, although she couldn't quite put her finger on what it was. But things had changed between her and Nick.

She supposed that was good. At least she'd come to know and understand the man who'd fathered her baby. And she liked him—as a person. He might be a little rough around the edges, but he had a tender side. She'd seen it when he gave in and rode the merry-go-round, something that probably hadn't been easy for a hard-edged cop.

Of course, the fact Nick hid a soft side and Hailey had come to see him in a different light still didn't change the obvious—they weren't suited and there could never be anything permanent or lasting between them. But at least she could tell her child that his or her father was a good man. A conscientious detective who wasn't cut out to be a dad, to be part of a family.

Nick stepped up behind her, placed a hand on her shoulder. "You've sure been pensive tonight."

She wanted to tilt her head, lay her cheek against his knuckles. Instead she turned, faced him. "There've been a lot of changes in my life."

He would probably assume she meant with Harry, and she did, to an extent. But the biggest change was the pregnancy and the growing attraction she felt toward her baby's father, a man who didn't fit into her carefully laid plans for a family of her own. A man who didn't even want to.

He caught her cheek in his hand, brushed his thumb across her skin, causing a warm flurry of tingles to race through her blood and settle low in her belly. His gaze lanced hers, slicing through the walls around her heart, opening old wounds and promising to heal them—at least momentarily. "You're a great lady, Hailey."

Was she?

She didn't feel so great. Not now. Not when she wanted to forget all her carefully laid plans and wrap her arms around the handsome detective who made her weak in the knees. Not when she wanted to pull him close, to convince them both that they should start right where they'd left off in Minnesota. To throw caution to the wind.

She desperately wanted to forget about the unexpected changes in her life, at least for the moment.

But did she dare?

You're a great lady, he had said. She wanted to be, at least in someone's eyes.

"I'm not anything special, Nick. I'm just trying to do the right thing. For me. For everyone involved." By everyone, she included the baby he didn't know about.

Would their son or daughter have his coffee-brown eyes? His crooked smile? His rebel spirit?

She hoped so, for some strange reason. Maybe so she could remember Nick, long after she'd gone back to Minnesota. But she made a conscious effort not to think about the future. Not tonight.

He bent his head to place a kiss on her lips, and she closed her eyes, leaned into him, accepting whatever he had to offer.

Nick took Hailey in his arms, giving in to the temptation to hold her again, abandoning all thoughts of right and wrong. He refused to think about tomorrow, about her returning to Minnesota, about where that would leave them. Where it might leave him.

Hailey triggered some weird, mushy feelings he'd never felt before. But he refused to focus on anything other than the taste of her kiss, the arousal building to mega proportions.

He ran his hands along her back, claiming each curve as his own, branding the feel of her into his memory.

As she leaned forward, pressed hard against his erection, matching his arousal with her own, she opened her mouth, allowing his tongue to sweep inside, to mate vigorously with hers.

He slipped a hand under her sweater, sought the heat of her skin, the softness of her breasts. And she lifted an arm, allowing him access. He'd never wanted a woman like this one, never wanted to make love so badly. To lose himself in her.

Had his arousal not been so strong, so mindless, he might have been scared spitless by what he felt for her. As it was, he had no choice but to take her to bed, to love her with his mouth, his hands. His body.

He palmed the lace-covered mound of her breast, then fumbled with the snap of her bra. A sense of urgency swept over him, and he fought the impulse to rip off her clothes in some primal, caveman-like way, to have her naked and writhing under him. To bury himself deep in her softness.

But he was a patient man—when he wanted to be. When he needed to be. And he intended to make love to Hailey with a slow hand. Even if it damn near killed him.

She pulled her mouth from his, her breath coming in short, ragged pants. "I know this isn't a good idea, and we may be sorry tomorrow—"

"Let's not think about tomorrow." Nick scooped

her into his arms and carried her behind the screen, to his bed. He let her slide the length of him, along the denim and metal buttons that held a demanding erection.

Passion glazed her eyes. He might not be a mind reader, but he could read her body. Sense her need.

And she wanted him, just as badly as he wanted her.

Hailey wasn't going to think about tomorrow, not until dawn brought a new day, a new worry. Tonight she would pretend that she and Nick had something special, something that neither of them would ever find with anyone else. In tonight's world of make-believe, they would hold forever in the palm of their hands.

She slipped the sweater over her head and dropped it to the floor, and as Nick watched, desire brewing in his gaze, she removed the bra that loosely covered her breasts.

"You're beautiful," he said, his voice laced with emotion—appreciation, sincerity.

Love?

Surely not, but she allowed herself the fantasy, the belief that what they were about to do, the joining, was right. A forever kind of thing, although she feared the only thing lasting would be the memory.

He unbuttoned his shirt, slipped it over his shoulders, baring his chest to her, and she ran her hands over the taut, corded muscles he must have worked hard to maintain. He sported a jagged scar near his left shoulder she hadn't noticed before. An old knife wound, she suspected, yet it didn't mar his good looks. Instead it added depth to his character, a hard edge that revealed he often challenged danger.

She reached for him, pressed her breasts against his chest, felt him skin to skin. "Love me," she whispered, the words taking all kinds of twists and turns that she wasn't about to contemplate. Not now.

And he did love her. With his hands, his mouth, his tongue.

When she didn't think she could take any more without having him inside her, he pulled away, but not before kissing her brow.

"We made a mistake last time," he said, reaching into the nightstand beside his bed and retrieving a condom. "I won't let that happen again."

Hailey nearly told him not to bother, that he didn't need to protect them from pregnancy. But she wasn't ready to reveal her secret. Wasn't ready to put a stop to their lovemaking, which a revelation like that was sure to do. Instead she bit her lip and watched as he unrolled the condom.

And after he'd made the unnecessary effort to protect them from pregnancy, he took her in his arms again, kissing her with a passion she'd never known. And when he laid her down on the bed and hovered over her, she forgot all about the secret she kept, all about the reasons why they could never become more than temporary lovers.

She wanted him now. Hard. Demanding. Yet he entered her slowly, as though savoring the moment, the warmth, the softness. The intimacy.

She arched up to meet him, and they were both lost in a swirl of heat, a rush of passion.

Like the very first time they'd made love, this joining was the kind that blazed a memory on the heart and soul.

In tandem, they both reached a mountainous crest. And in the blink of an eye, the beat of a heart, they climaxed in a star-spinning, earth-shattering burst of fulfillment that carried them to a faraway place, a place where intimacy thrived.

And when the last wave of pleasure passed, they held on to each other, as though afraid to lose contact, to lose what they'd found in each other's arms.

Yet, as much as Hailey would like to cling to Nick, to a relationship with him, the memory of their lovemaking would have to be enough.

Because Nick had made himself clear.

He wasn't daddy material.

And he didn't want to be.

Chapter Eleven

Nick held Hailey throughout the night, drawing comfort from the apricot scent of her shampoo, from the gentle rise and fall of her chest.

Not a cuddler by nature, his need to keep her close during sleep surprised him, as did the contentment he felt at having her near. In fact, with her bottom cradled in his lap and his arm draped across her breast, he rested better than he had in ages.

Until the alarm clock blasted a rude wake-up call.

Nick rolled to the side, away from Hailey, and fumbled with the button on the old-style, windup clock he always used. Technology might be great in many respects, but some things couldn't be improved upon—like knowing the damn alarm would work even if the electricity went out.

Hailey, eyes still closed, arched her back and yawned. "It doesn't feel like morning."

He brushed a tendril of hair from her face and kissed her cheek. "Time to get up, sleepyhead."

"I know."

Harry's surgery was scheduled for eight that morning, and if they arrived early enough, they could see him before he was wheeled through the O.R. doors.

"Want me to shower first?" he asked. "Or should I go down to the corner for coffee?"

She tugged at the sheets, pulling them up to her chin, then rolled over, making her answer known. "Don't forget my tea."

He had a feeling she'd use the time to lie in bed, rather than shower. If not for the upcoming surgery, he wouldn't mind if she stayed in his bed all day. He started to kiss her again, but thought better of it. When had he begun having such sappy feelings?

It had to be the sex. He'd never had a lover who turned him inside out. Who made him want to stay in bed longer than was emotionally savvy.

Yeah. That was it.

He raked a hand through his hair. "We need to leave in about twenty minutes."

"I'll be ready," she said, before placing a pillow over her head.

He didn't know how long it would take for her to do the things women did to get dressed, but he figured the hardest part would be getting mentally ready. Maybe that's what she hoped to do while he was gone, what she was doing now, cocooned in his bed. He hoped so.

Because today would prove to be stressful for them both.

Not only did Nick worry about his old friend and mentor, he also wanted to stand by Hailey, offer her his support. His friendship.

It was the least he could do for her.

True to her word, she was up and in the shower when he returned with the coffee and tea. And an hour later, they entered Harry's hospital room.

The old detective smiled, and his eyes lit up. Happy to see them, no doubt.

But would Harry be happy to know his daughter and the guy he'd taken under his wing had spent most of the night making love? It had never been easy to pull a fast one on Harry. The detective was too sharp, too instinctive.

"So," Harry said. "You two look chipper."

Did he suspect they'd become lovers?

Nick shoved his hands into the front pockets of his jeans. "I've always been a morning person."

"Not me," Hailey said.

Another difference between them, Nick supposed.

"I hope you got a chance to see San Diego," Harry said. Nick wondered if he also hoped Hailey would like the harbor town, consider visiting more often. Maybe even move here.

But Harry hadn't seen her house in Walden, the little place she'd made into home.

No, Nick didn't think she'd be willing to give that place up. He wouldn't, if he were her. Well, he wouldn't if he needed a nest like that.

"Nick showed me the sights yesterday," Hailey said. "He even rode the Balboa Park merry-go-round with me."

"He did?" Harry shot him one of those You-did-what? looks.

Nick merely shrugged, hoping word of this didn't reach the precinct. If any of the guys found out, he'd never hear the end of it.

"And that's not all," Hailey said, causing Nick to squirm.

His thoughts immediately flew to last night, to the lovemaking. Nah, she wouldn't mention that. Not to her dad.

"He took me to Old Town, where we sat and listened to the mariachis."

"Sounds kind of romantic," Harry said.

"No, it doesn't," Nick countered, a bit louder and sharper than necessary. "I was just being a nice guy and taking her places you would have taken her, if you could have."

"Nick's a nice guy, all right." Hailey gave Nick a look he found hard to decipher, then slid her father a smile.

They chatted for a while, then Hailey and Nick wished Harry well. As they left the room, a nurse's aid passed by with a cart of breakfast trays. The scent of hospital food filled the air.

Nick was about to guide Hailey to the waiting room, when she muttered, ''Nervous stomach.''

Then she quickly excused herself and rushed down the hall.

Just after Harry had been wheeled into surgery, Hailey excused herself from Nick's side, intending to slip into the bathroom again.

''Are you sick?'' Nick had asked, concern and disbelief mingling on his face.

''No,'' she'd quickly answered. ''Just a sensitive stomach when stressed.''

Apparently, he'd believed her. Thank goodness. There was no way she wanted the detective to suspect the real reason for her nausea.

''You want me to wait outside for you?'' he'd asked, as she neared the bathroom.

''Go on and join the others. I'll just be a minute.'' Then she ducked behind the rest room door and quickly chose an empty stall. When the heaving ceased, she splashed her face with cool water and blotted it dry.

Her tummy temporarily settled, Hailey stood in the entryway of the waiting room.

The walls were a soft shade of green and adorned with strips of floral-printed wallpaper that added a homey touch. Overstuffed sofas and love seats, upholstered in coordinating patterns, had been strategically placed, creating small, intimate areas. And, as an added touch, fresh flowers and plants on oak tables provided a cozy charm.

The decorator, it seemed, had tried to create a comfortable place for people to await the outcome of a loved one's surgery. Yet Hailey didn't feel any calming effects. Her nerves were on high alert.

And her stomach was a mess.

Morning sickness, intensified by a severe case of anxiety and stress, had sent her scurrying to the ladies' room several times.

She glanced at her watch: 8:27. According to the word Nick had received, Harry's surgery was expected to take three to four hours, which would make for an interminably long wait.

Keenly aware of her personal discomfort and stress, Hailey had to admit, deep in her heart, she also worried about the fate of the man who had fathered her, the police officer who'd let her climb into his patrol car when she was a child. The man who had more than once brought her a small container of chocolate milk and a jelly-filled doughnut as a treat because he knew how much she liked chocolate and raspberries.

The memories, she supposed, had been good. At least while they lasted.

Before she could find an obscure spot in which she could blend into a shadowed corner, Harry's wife led several people her way. "Hailey, I'd like you to meet your brothers and their families."

Brothers?

She'd only meant to meet with Harry, to let him think things had been resolved between them, but after seeing him in that hospital bed and hearing his side of the story, she'd weakened.

And now as she studied the four new faces of people who claimed the same shaky branch of her family tree, trepidation washed over her.

Hailey brushed her moist palms down her denim-covered thighs before she considered shaking anyone's hand.

"This is Daniel, our middle son." Kay lovingly stroked the tall, lanky man's shoulder and smiled. "Dan's an industrial engineer and lives in Los Angeles."

Dan Logan, a slightly balding man in his late thirties, took Hailey's hand in his, giving it a gentle squeeze. "It's nice to meet you."

Was it? Hailey couldn't help but question his sincerity, even though a gentle smile graced his face—a face that boasted blue eyes remarkably similar to his mother's.

"It's nice to meet you, too." Hailey wished the words hadn't sounded so stilted, so rehearsed. Yet she wasn't sure why. The greeting was merely a standard response. Had she wanted to come up with something better?

Dan turned to a towheaded teenage boy wearing a blue-and-white letterman's jacket. The stocky kid looked to be about sixteen, more or less. "This is my son, Eric."

Hailey shook hands with the teenager and offered him a smile, which he shyly returned.

Gosh, this was hard. Awkward. Weird. She struggled with a mishmash of emotions, particularly curiosity and a bit of skepticism.

Unable to help herself, she glanced across the room, needing a lifeline, a touchstone. Needing Nick.

She found him near the television, talking to a man wearing a minister's collar. Nick's eyes locked on hers, offering something—support? Strength?

She wasn't sure what she'd seen in his gaze, but she clung to it just the same and found a comfort she hadn't expected.

"And this," Kay said, drawing Hailey's attention back to the introductions, "is our youngest son, Joseph."

A sandy-haired man, also in his thirties, stepped forward and slid Hailey a smile. His face held a rugged, weathered look, suggesting he spent more time outdoors than his brother did.

Kay placed a hand on her son's back, maternal pride apparent in her smile. "Our boys have done very well for themselves. Joe's a grading contractor and owns a construction company in Tucson."

Joe Logan greeted Hailey, then turned to an attractive brunette. "This is my wife, Maria."

"Mucho gusto." The petite woman's green eyes indicated sincerity. "Welcome to the family."

"Thank you." It seemed like the right response, yet Hailey wasn't sure whether she wanted to be accepted by these people or not.

The men, although pleasant, seemed to assess her with a critical eye. Were they trying to determine what kind of problem their illegitimate half sister would present to the family? Or had they merely spotted the resemblance to their oldest brother who had died?

Hailey wasn't sure, but she offered a polite smile and some small talk before excusing herself. Then she quickly chose a seat in the far corner of the room, away from the door or the television. Away from the path most folks would wander.

Hailey might be Harry's daughter, biologically speaking, but she really wasn't part of the Logan family. Not yet. And she still wasn't sure whether she wanted to be.

Yet curiosity nagged at her, and she couldn't help but study the people in the room.

Several younger men stood in clusters—a fireman in uniform with a radio on his hip, a guy in a snazzy three-piece suit. Another in faded jeans and a Harley Davidson shirt. They all appeared to be part of the Logan group.

Were they the guys both Nick and Kay had mentioned, the ones who'd once been delinquents Harry had befriended? Guys like Nick who felt an allegiance to the retired detective?

She again sought the man who'd brought her here, caught him watching her. He seemed to excuse himself before making his way through the crowd, shaking hands with people along the way. Yet his focus remained on her.

Hailey welcomed his presence. His strength. His support.

When he took the seat next to her, she leaned toward him and whispered, "Who are all these people?"

"Harry's co-workers. Kay's church friends. Neighbors." He flashed her a crooked grin. "And most of the guys who turned their sorry lives around because of the efforts of a kindhearted but stubborn cop. I'll introduce you to them when you're ready."

Hailey didn't think she'd ever be ready. Yet she couldn't help but feel a sense of pride in her father, a man who provided a fine example to so many guys who might otherwise have ended up on the wrong side of the law.

The men, now grown and their lives on track, seemed to comfort Kay. As did Hailey's two half brothers.

Dan and Joe Logan appeared to have accepted her as a family member. Her sister-in-law had, too. It both pleased her and placed an additional burden on her heart. How much of a relationship did she want with these people?

Hailey snagged a magazine off the table and flipped through the pages, trying to ignore the comings and goings of people in the room. But when a handsome yet sober-faced doctor dressed in a white lab coat entered and strode toward Kay, Hailey's heart thumped to her stomach.

It was too early. The surgery was supposed to last much longer than this. Had something gone wrong? Had Harry...died?

The young doctor greeted Kay first, giving her a hug.

Hailey elbowed Nick and leaned toward him. "Who's that?"

"It's Luke," he said. "Dr. Lucas Wynter, I mean. Another one of Logan's Heroes."

She studied the young doctor, then slid a glance at the one-time bad boy sitting beside her, caught his profile, the square cut of his chin, the angular cheekbones. Something told her there was still a bit of rebel in the detective, something she found far more appealing than she should.

Don't get too close, her conscience ordered. *Nick Granger may be easy to lean on today, but he's not the kind of man you want or need.*

And he wasn't.

Even if he did happen to be her temporary lover.

And the father of her baby.

Like the others, Nick stood when the cardiovascular surgeon finally entered the waiting room and announced that Harry had made it through surgery and had been taken to recover in ICU.

The room, once filled with tension, eased as smiles, happy tears and hugs prevailed.

After saying goodbye to Kay, Nick took Hailey by the hand. "Come on. Let's get out of here."

For some reason, he thought she might resist him taking the lead, but she clung to his hand, making him feel like some kind of hero and protector, and followed him down the corridor that led to the hospital entrance.

No doubt she was eager to escape. The long,

stressful wait had done a real number on her, he supposed, especially since she'd spent so much time in the bathroom.

He had a feeling she'd puked her guts out earlier, because each time she'd come out of the john, she'd appeared pale. Drained.

Thank God his nerves didn't react like hers.

As they left the hospital, Nick expected Hailey to let go of his hand, but surprisingly, she held on tight.

It felt weird but good to hold her close, to lead her out of the hospital, to help her escape a stress-filled day.

With each step they took, she seemed to gain strength. Probably from the fresh air, but it felt kind of nice to think his presence had something to do with it.

When they reached the parking lot, she asked, "Where are we going?"

"I'm taking you home."

Home. It seemed like the perfect place for them to go to unwind. To relax. To be together.

"Unless you'd rather go somewhere else," he added.

"No, that's fine, but can you slow down? I'm a bit light-headed."

Good grief, she wasn't going to faint on him again, was she? He'd had emergency training and could perform CPR in his sleep, if need be, but the thought of Hailey passed out on the ground didn't sit well with him.

His steps slowed to a stop. "You gonna be okay?"

"Yes, I think so." She offered him a weak smile. "If you don't make me dash through the parking lot like a running back dodging opponents."

"Sorry," he said, resuming a slower trek to the Jeep.

Although glad to be out of the limelight, Hailey pondered the changes that this morning had brought. The people who'd been introduced to her, family members, if she wanted to claim them.

She thought about Harry, her father. And Kay. Siblings who had become real, rather than faceless creatures who'd claimed her father when she was only six. She also had a sister-in-law. A nephew.

How would they all fit into her life? Into her baby's life?

She slid a glance at Nick, at his rugged profile. Was there a place in her life for a man like him? For the father of her baby?

He opened the passenger door for her, then proceeded to the driver's side and climbed in. Within minutes they were heading back home.

Or rather to Nick's place.

"When are you scheduled to fly back to Minnesota?" he asked.

"I have an open ticket." She could go home whenever she wanted to.

He seemed to ponder her answer. "How long do you think you'll stay?"

"I'm not sure. I'd planned on going home tomorrow." Of course, that was before meeting her brothers. Before she considered being part of Harry's family—not that she'd made a decision yet.

"Are you saying your plans are still up in the air?"

Well, sort of. She didn't have to be back to work until next week, should she decide to stay longer.

She slid a glance at Nick, trying to read his stoical expression. Did he want her to stay? Did it even matter to him on a personal level?

"What do you think I ought to do?" she asked, but after the words left her mouth she wanted to reel them back in.

As much as she wanted to know what Nick was thinking about their hot but destined-to-be-brief love affair, she didn't want him to think she was…she was what?

Taking things to a more intimate and personal level?

A part of her wanted to. But not the rational, organized part. "Let me rephrase that question. Do you think I should stay an extra day or two, just to make sure Harry is okay?"

Nick really shouldn't give a damn when she went back to Minnesota, as long as she and Harry had a chance to meet and reconcile. But for some reason he did.

Because of the sex, he told himself. That's why he wasn't ready for her to go. Because once she boarded that plane, their relationship—or whatever it was they had—would be over.

"I'm sure Harry will want to see you," he said, "once he's out of ICU."

"You're right." She glanced out the window of the car, studying the coastline as they headed south on Interstate 5. A moment or two later, she turned her head, caught his eye. "You don't mind if I stay with you?"

He shot her a crooked smile. "Not unless you send me back to the sofa to sleep."

"I ought to."

"Why is that?" he asked, willing to discuss the merits of a no-strings involved relationship while she was in San Diego.

"Because I think a relationship should be based upon more than sexual compatibility."

"I guess it should be," he said, "if a relationship had any chance of lasting."

She nodded, then looked out at the ocean again, staring at the horizon long after the freeway wound inland and the Pacific was lost from view.

Had he hurt her feelings? He hoped not. But Nick Granger wasn't cut out for the kind of relationship Hailey wanted or needed. The kind of relationship that promised commitment and love. The kind that promised the happily-ever-after found in storybooks.

Nick was a realist.

But for the first time in his life, he was almost sorry that he was.

Chapter Twelve

Later that afternoon, Nick and Hailey went back to the hospital to see Harry. They stayed only long enough to let him know they were there, then left his bedside.

"He looks good," Hailey said, "Better than I expected."

Nick didn't know about that. There were a few too many tubes and wires still hooked up to the once-rugged cop to suit him, but at least Harry's color was better. And he was talking, smiling even. That sure counted for something.

"The nurse said they'll move him to an intermediate care floor tomorrow, if he continues to improve." Nick ushered Hailey out of ICU, and the big, double doors locked behind them.

A waiting room for those visiting someone in Intensive Care sat to the left. Nick ushered Hailey inside so they could give their regards to Kay. There weren't nearly as many friends and supporters at the hospital as there had been this morning, but Nick suspected Harry still had more visitors than the norm.

Once in the room they mingled. Nick spoke to Joe Davenport, a man who had become a good friend. He'd met the fireman a few years back at a Logan family barbecue and found they'd shared more than Harry and a crappy childhood. They'd both loved surfing, and a friendship naturally developed. As always, it was good to see Joe, but Nick couldn't keep his gaze from wandering, from searching for Hailey.

Fortunately, she appeared to be more at ease this evening. More confident.

At least she hadn't gotten that stupid nervous stomach that sent her to the ladies' room off and on. In fact, she chatted awhile with both of her brothers, and if the smiles were any indication, they'd all begun to accept their new relationship.

When Hailey walked to the water cooler in the corner, Nick joined her. She filled a paper cup, then offered it to him. The thoughtfulness of her gesture touched him, even though anyone else might think of it as no big deal.

But people hadn't always put Nick's needs first, including his mom who'd sometimes been too drunk to cook breakfast, let alone dinner, and a stepdad who didn't care if his stepson ate or not. For a guy who, when growing up, had to muscle in and take what he wanted, what he needed, Nick hadn't always had such consideration from others—not until Harry came along.

He really wasn't thirsty, but he took the paper cup from her. "Thanks."

Hailey got a drink for herself, then scanned the smiling faces. "I'm surprised at how many people are still here."

"Harry and Kay are good people. They have a lot of friends. And I imagine folks have been coming and going all day."

"Do you think we should leave?" she asked. "Maybe come back tomorrow?"

"It's probably a good idea." But Nick wasn't just thinking about weeding out the crowd. He was thinking about getting Hailey home, about spending a quiet evening with her. About ending it in bed. Together. Making love and waking with her in his arms again.

He suspected there wouldn't be many more chances for them to be together again, not once she boarded that Minnesota-bound plane.

Which would be too bad, he realized, a twinge of regret socking him in the chest. He'd gotten kind of used to having her around. Surprisingly.

It was the sex, he reminded himself. A good lover was hard to find. And Hailey was better than good.

He crushed the paper cup in his hand, then dropped it into the trash. And after a few parting words to Kay, he and Hailey left the hospital.

"Do you think you can find this place by yourself?" he asked.

"If I had to. Why?"

"I've got to go to work in the morning. But if you drop me off at the precinct, you can use the Jeep."

She paused, brow furrowed, pondering something. Whether she could handle coming alone? Whether she could find her way without him? He wasn't sure.

"Will you draw me a map?" she asked. "Just in case?"

"Sure." Nick glanced across the seat, momentarily wishing he had the kind of job that would allow him to take more time off. But he didn't. And it was crazy to even think about it. He wouldn't want another job if given the chance. Being a detective suited him. Gave him a satisfaction he couldn't get anywhere else.

Hailey didn't say anything, just took his announcement about work in stride. Had they been married or had some other kind of live-in-type arrangement, he figured she might have voiced a complaint. Whined. Demanded more of him. The way Carla had.

It was, he supposed, just one more reason why it was good she was leaving, heading back to Minnesota when Harry's surgery was behind them.

Yet, thinking about Hailey leaving didn't sit well with him. Not at all. And that twinge in his chest tightened. Vise-like.

It's the sex, he again reminded himself. A guy could get damned used to having a woman like

Hailey warm his bed. A lady who turned him every which way but loose, who made him think about sleeping with her, even when the sun was shining and she was nowhere in sight.

"How about we pick up some Chinese take-out," he suggested, trying to keep his thoughts on track. On getting home, eating and having sex. Nothing sappy or sentimental. "There's a great little place in Hillcrest called Johnny Wong's. I can call ahead. Then maybe we can kick off our shoes, relax. What do you say?"

"A quiet evening sounds good," she said. "It's been a trying day."

It had. And Nick was ready to unwind. To curl up on the bed and make love to Hailey all night long. Especially since they didn't have too many more nights together.

Once again, as he thought of putting her on that plane and sending her back to Minnesota, back to that little house in Walden, where the fire flickered in the hearth, where the pot roast juices simmered in the oven, where the scent of lavender permeated the sheets and teased a guy's senses…

Nick swore under his breath.

He hadn't been born into a life like that, hadn't ever wanted one. Didn't want one now.

But he suspected letting Hailey go back where she belonged might be a hell of a lot tougher than it should be.

And he really wasn't looking forward to it.

* * *

The city lights mingled with twinkling stars, casting a romantic spell on the patio where Nick and Hailey sat.

Back home, Hailey wouldn't even consider stargazing while eating sweet-and-sour pork, fried rice and chicken chow mein by candlelight in early January. But here, in southern California, where the night was a little cool, it was still pleasant.

She had to admit, though, part of the appeal was the handsome detective who sat across from her, fumbling with a pair of chopsticks.

She lifted her fork, twirled it in her hand and smiled. ''Want me to get you one of these? They're much easier to master.''

''Heck, no. The food tastes better this way. Besides,'' he said, offering her a cocky smile, ''practice makes perfect. And I'm no quitter.''

She didn't suppose he was. There was so much more to Nick Granger than met the eye, so much he kept locked deep inside. That dark, secretive and pensive nature made him a good cop, she suspected.

He reached for a clump of rice, dropping half of it back onto the paper plate and scattering it over his chow mein.

There was something sweet about the guy, something even her persnickety side couldn't fault.

She tried to focus on the many reasons why happily-ever-after wasn't in their future. Why a relationship should be based on more than great sex. Why her child would be better off growing up in a small town, rather than a big city.

But it just didn't seem to matter tonight, not with the splatter of city lights and sparkling stars decorating a mild winter sky. Not with the candlelight flickering and drawing her into a romantic evening, the likes of which she'd never had before and—more than likely—never would again.

Nick glanced across the table and slid her that crooked grin she could grow used to seeing. "What are you thinking about?"

"Nothing." Nothing that matters right now.

He took a swig from a long-neck bottle of beer, his eyes never leaving hers. "Want to talk about it?"

"Talk about nothing?" she asked, still not willing to admit anything was on her mind.

"Or whatever you're holding back."

Nope. Not that. Not yet. She wasn't ready to upset the little raft she drifted upon. The minute she told Nick about the baby, he'd tense. Pull back. Remind her he wasn't a family man, that he didn't want kids.

But, if slapped in the face with the reality of a child, would he change his mind?

Did she feel like taking the gamble?

As long as she kept her secret, she still had the option to turn tail and run back to Minnesota, to raise her child without any interference. To find a stepfather who would be the kind of daddy her baby deserved. To create a loving family of her own.

For goodness sake, she'd only known about the pregnancy for a couple of weeks. It was early yet.

She hadn't begun to show, hadn't even seen a doctor—which reminded her, she had to make an appointment as soon as she got home.

"You've got something weighing on your mind," Nick said. "I can see it in your eyes."

"I guess I'm just thinking about the future."

"That's reasonable, I suppose."

She placed her fork on her plate. "I'll be going back to Minnesota soon. Where does that leave us?"

The question seemed to hang in the air, suspended from the stars above, at least for a moment. But she doubted it was because the question hadn't crossed his mind, too. But like her, she supposed he'd avoided putting it into words.

"We both sort of slipped into this, knowing that there wasn't any future for us," he said.

"I know."

Nick reached across the table, took her hand in his. "You need a home and a family. Not a loner like me."

Yeah. She did need a home, a husband. A family. But deep inside she wondered if the loner needed her.

No. Not wondered. She *knew* he needed her, or someone like her. A lover or maybe even a wife. But she also knew better than to try to convince him a happy home was something of value, something everyone needed. She'd tried that one time too many, back when she'd wanted desperately for her mother to appreciate home, hearth and a loving daughter.

Hailey had learned an important lesson back then, one she'd never forget: when the coach wanted a win more than the team did, the game was over before it started.

"I care for you, Hailey. More than I intended to."

And she cared for him, too. Way more than she expected. Way more than was prudent. "Same here, Nick."

"I guess we just need to make the best of what we have, here and now."

He was right, she supposed. And what they did have, a friendship of sorts, was enhanced by an incredible sexual relationship. Temporary, but amazing just the same.

He adjusted the chopsticks and went after another clump of fried rice.

She glanced at her plate, no longer hungry, then looked across the table, saw a grain of rice on his chin and smiled. She leaned forward and brushed it away for him, her fingers snagging on his lightly bristled jaw. And lingering there.

He caught her hand, brought her fingers to his lips and kissed her palm. His gaze, darkened by desire, snagged hers, drawing her into the depths, into him, consuming all her worries and fears—at least for the time being.

Heat pooled low in her belly, as her passion brewed, matching his.

Without words, without needing to use them, he stood and took her hand, leading her into the house.

They left the remainder of their dinner, the paper plates and cartons, on the patio table. They left the future there, too. Outside with the table scraps and litter, out of sight. Out of mind.

Once in the privacy of Nick's home, they embraced the here and now, their kisses hot, their hands stroking, caressing.

They made love as though it might be their last time, their last chance, which it well could be. And the union was both mind-spinning and bittersweet.

As Hailey held on to Nick, accepting the only love he had to offer, she closed her eyes and enjoyed the best lovemaking she'd ever experienced, the best she probably ever would.

But there was more to life than magic between the sheets.

And Hailey wanted more. Much more than Nick was willing to give.

After Nick gave Hailey his Thomas Brothers' map to help her navigate around town and directions from the precinct to the hospital, Hailey dropped him off at work.

Then she drove to Oceana General Hospital to see Harry.

Her father.

A warmth settled in her heart, a coziness that had been missing for a very long time.

She entered the lobby, then stopped by the front desk where volunteers waited to point people in the right direction.

"I've come to see Harry Logan," she said. "Is he still in ICU?"

"I'll check," a silver-haired woman in a pink smock said. "No, he's now in Room 314."

"Thank you." Hailey started for the elevator, then stopped in front of the gift shop doors. For some reason, she hated to go into Harry's room empty-handed.

She quickly decided against flowers—the man would probably get a ton. And chocolate—the doctor had probably restricted his diet. And a stuffed animal.

So, why did she linger before that display, caressing a floppy-eared purple bunny and having wistful thoughts of a diapered little cherub with a toothless grin?

She shook off the baby sentiment and continued to shop, settling upon a small, silver picture frame.

After paying the woman behind the counter, she carried her bag to the third floor. When she entered Harry's room, she saw that Kay sat in the chair beside him.

"Hey," her father said from his hospital bed, eyes lighting up in recognition.

A smile graced Kay's face. "Hailey, I'm so glad you came."

And the truth was Hailey was glad, too.

"Hi," she said to Harry. And as a second thought, or an attempt to reach out, she added, "Dad."

His eyes watered and a single tear spilled onto his cheek. He brushed it aside with a beefy hand. "I'm going to spend the rest of my life trying to make things up to you, honey."

"That's okay," she told him, meaning the words, but pleased that he wanted to make things right between them. "I've got some making up to do, too."

"I wish you didn't have to leave, that you'd consider sticking around longer. Maybe...well, you know."

She figured he was hoping she'd move to San Diego, take part in their family. "We can renew a relationship without me living next door."

"Yeah," the burly old cop said. "I know that. But if you need anything, anything at all, I want you to call me. I'll be there for you, Hailey. From now on."

"Thanks, Dad. I really appreciate that."

And she did.

She'd come to San Diego without expecting anything from Harry. What she'd received was love, warmth and acceptance. And in spite of her determination to remain aloof, on her own, she began to feel like a Logan. Like part of Harry's family.

But it wasn't enough. What about her baby?

Would Harry and Kay accept the child, a fatherless little boy or girl, as readily as they accepted Hailey?

She truly believed they would. But she held her tongue, her secret, unsure of how or when to reveal the news. Instead she handed Harry the paper bag. "It's not much, but I brought you something."

Her father withdrew the frame, looked at it a bit quizzically, maybe because it still boasted the manufactured photograph of strangers.

"I thought that...well, maybe...I could send you a picture of me. And maybe you could put it up on the mantel.'' She shot a glance at Kay. ''I mean, if that's where you keep your photos. And if it's all right—''

Kay stood and wrapped her arms around Hailey, drew her near with a comforting hug that enveloped her in a scent of springtime. ''We'd love to display your photograph with the others, right in front. And if you'll send us more than one, after you get home, I'll put them in some new frames and place them throughout the house.''

''Thanks,'' Hailey said, her voice threatening to crack. ''I'll do that.''

When I get home.

But for some reason, her little house no longer seemed quite as appealing as it once had. Not if she had to return and raise her baby without a family.

Kay released her, then reached into her purse and withdrew a small notepad and pen. ''Here's our phone number and address. Please call us or come by—anytime—while you're in town, or after you get home. It doesn't matter. We'd love to hear from you even if it's just to chat and let us know how you are.''

''I will. Thanks.'' Hailey gave Harry a kiss on the cheek and squeezed his hand. ''I've got to get going.''

If he suspected that she didn't have anywhere to go, anything pressing to do, he didn't mention it.

''Thanks for coming by,'' he said. ''I'll see you again, won't I? Before you leave.''

"Of course you will. I won't go without saying goodbye."

Then she slipped out of the hospital room, unsure of any particular destination, but aware of a need to be alone, to think.

She placed a hand in her pocket, felt the folded slip of paper she'd put there. The paper bearing Harry and Kay's address and phone number.

Once she'd gone through the lobby and out the revolving glass doors, she exhaled a shaky breath.

The time was coming. She'd soon have to make some kind of decision regarding her baby and the announcement of her pregnancy.

As she reached the row of vehicles in which she'd parked the Jeep, she spotted a young couple getting out of their Nissan Sentra. The woman took a toddler out of a car seat in back, while the man removed a stroller from the trunk and set it up.

A darling little boy with dark hair, pudgy cheeks and a happy grin said, "Me want Daddy to push."

"That's my boy," the man said, flashing the woman a pearly white smile.

Hailey couldn't help but try to imagine Nick at her side, helping her with their little boy, taking an active part in their son's life.

But he'd told her he didn't want a family.

And even if he did, what kind of husband and father would he make? He'd never be home. Hailey would be coaching soccer herself on the weekends. And going to parent-teacher conferences and school programs all by herself.

The tears began to stream down her face, and she swiped at them with the back of her hand.

She'd be raising their child alone.

Well, not alone, she realized, glancing at the ten-story hospital behind her.

Harry and Kay might want to play an active role in her baby's life. Again her hand sought the folded paper in her pocket as though it was a talisman. For the first time, she began to feel a sense of hope. A sense that everything would work out for the best.

Maybe having a loving mother and grandparents would be enough for her baby.

She hoped so.

Because that's all she could provide, all she could count on.

Chapter Thirteen

Nick called Hailey and told her he'd be late coming home. A lead in a new case had struck pay dirt, and he and his partner had to hit the streets.

"Don't wait up for me," he said.

"I won't."

Still, disappointment settled around her. She'd picked up groceries and cooked a meal, nothing special. Just a meat loaf and baked potatoes. Fresh green beans and almonds. A fruit salad with a lemon yogurt dressing.

Okay, so she'd wanted to surprise him with a nice dinner. It had been a dumb thing to do, anyway, because she suspected Nick's idea of a good meal was probably fast food and take-out.

"Are you going to be able to find something to eat?" he asked.

She glanced at the pot of green beans on the stove, the cloverleaf rolls she'd intended to pop in the oven as soon as the meat and potatoes were done. "I'll manage to find something."

"And don't worry about coming to get me," he added. "I'll catch a ride home with my partner."

"All right." She tucked a strand of hair behind her ear.

This was the kind of disappointment she could expect, if she and Nick were married.

Married? To Nick? What a silly notion. That was the kind of senseless fantasy little girls dreamed up when they played with their Barbie and Ken dolls on the bedroom floor.

She scanned the apartment, which had remained tidy after she'd cleaned, other than the towels Nick continued to mess up in the bathroom. What was so tough about keeping them hanging evenly?

His disregard for neatness irritated her some, but she merely straightened the towels each time he took a shower or used the bathroom.

She slipped her hand into the pocket of her jeans and withdrew the folded paper Kay had given her. She fingered it like a lucky rabbit's foot. For some reason it seemed like a tangible piece of evidence that she belonged. That she had someone who cared about her. That she was part of a family.

"Don't worry if I don't come home at all tonight," Nick said.

"I won't," she lied, knowing she would, even though she really didn't have any right to worry, since it wasn't her place. But she'd watched enough television shows and movies about cops and detectives to realize the dangers that lurked in the city after the law-abiding citizens went to sleep. And just knowing that Nick would be out on the streets at that time stirred her fears, made them rise to the surface. Other things rose to the surface, too. Heart-touching things she had no business contemplating.

"Take care of yourself," he said.

"You, too."

The line was silent for a while, as though there were things that still needed to be said, as though they both clung to some lame reason to stay connected.

Or maybe that was just her overactive, romantic imagination, wishing they had a bond that would last.

Either way, he was the first to say goodbye.

And for some stupid reason, she held on to the receiver longer than necessary.

When the annoying beep-beep-beep sounded, alerting her to the dead connection, she hung up and dialed the number Kay had given her. The older woman answered on the third ring.

"Hi, Kay. It's me, Hailey."

"Well, hello, dear."

That was Hailey's cue to say something, to respond, to tell Kay why she called. Instead she held the receiver, her lips frozen in silence like a stage-struck understudy.

Nope. Not over the phone. Some things needed to be said in person.

"Would it be all right if I came by to see you?" Hailey asked, then quickly interjected, "Not tonight, of course. But maybe tomorrow?"

"Certainly. What time would you like to stop by?"

After agreeing upon ten o'clock the next morning and getting some verbal directions to further explain the address she'd already been given, Hailey told Kay goodbye and hung up the phone.

Alone again.

But not for long. She had a family.

Of course, that was assuming Kay Logan didn't have a problem with the illegitimate child of an illegitimate child.

The next morning, at five minutes after ten, Hailey sat across an oval antique oak table in Kay's breakfast nook, a cheery little sitting area with pale-lavender walls and a large bay window framed by a valance of Irish lace.

A pot of tea and two delicate china cups with pink carnation trim sat before them, as did a matching creamer and sugar bowl and a plate of oatmeal cookies.

It was the kind of setting little girls who liked dressing up and having tea parties dreamed about. The kind Hailey had always imagined.

She noticed the functional kitchen—cheerful, with a wallpaper border of violets. The white countertops boasted all the appliances a woman who loved to cook would need. "You have a beautiful home."

"Thank you."

Hailey glanced out the window, into a moderate-size yard filled with plants, ferns and palm trees—each one trimmed neatly. It amazed her to see flowers blooming in winter, especially since Minnesota was so cold and barren. On the patio, a built-in barbecue grill sat amidst redwood furniture. She could easily imagine an outdoor party, with Nick and the guys hanging around the grill, Kay making everyone feel welcome.

"Did you just want to chat, to get to know each other better?" Kay asked. "Or is there something on your mind?"

Hailey looked up and caught the woman's kind smile. "Yes, there's something I need to tell you. Harry...I mean my dad, too. But I thought I'd practice on you, if that's okay."

"A burden is more easily carried by two."

Was it that obvious? That she had a burden, a dilemma?

Hailey fiddled with the edge of her napkin, then looked up at Kay, hoping she'd read the woman right. "I'm expecting a baby."

Kay's teacup seemed to stop in midair, neither going up nor down.

Was she shocked? Surprised?

The older woman searched Hailey's face, her eyes, as though looking for something, although Hailey didn't know what.

"Why don't I sense a feeling of happiness?" Kay asked.

Hailey blew out a sigh. "It's not that I don't want a child, but I'm not married. And this is not how I'd intended to start a family."

"And the father? How does he feel about it?"

The father.

For some reason Hailey had hoped to sidestep that little complication by announcing him missing in action. But that wasn't entirely the truth, was it?

Nick hadn't bailed out. Yet.

"He, uh, doesn't know about it. And I'm not looking forward to telling him."

Kay lifted her cup and took a sip of tea. "Are you afraid of his reaction?"

"Yes, for more reasons than one. The pregnancy came as a surprise to me. I've always wanted to be a mother, someday. The timing, of course, could certainly be better."

"And you don't think the father will be pleased to learn about the baby?"

Hailey slowly shook her head. "He told me that he wasn't cut out to be a husband or a father."

"Well," Kay said, reaching a hand across the table. "Expecting a baby should be a time of joy and happiness. Let's find something we can celebrate."

Hailey hadn't thought to look on the bright side, hadn't even thought there was one.

"Children are a blessing," Kay said. "And I'm happy for you. Harry and I love babies. And we'd be happy to help you in any way we can."

Tears filled Hailey's eyes, and she quickly swiped them away, as though she didn't want Kay to know how touched she was by the offer. The support. The understanding. "Thank you. It's going to be rough, raising a child alone, that's for sure. Especially since I'll have to get a sitter while I work, and that wasn't an expense I'd budgeted for."

"I'm not sure how long you plan to be in San Diego, but we have a guest room. You're more than welcome to stay with us. Or to come back whenever you want."

"I'd like that," Hailey said. And she would. More than she'd ever thought possible.

But reality struck hard.

If she intended to be part of the Logan family, to bring her baby to visit, she couldn't keep the secret from Nick. Not anymore.

The guy might not be up on the symptoms of early pregnancy, but he could count.

Would he be angry? Sullen?

Once she told him, she might not be welcome to stay at his place any longer. In fact, she might not want to.

"Would you mind if I stayed here for a day or two?" she asked Kay.

"Not at all. I'll show you the guest room, then get you a key. If I'm not home, you can let yourself in."

"Thank you."

The time had come. Hailey would tell Nick.

Then face the consequences, whatever they might be.

* * *

When Hailey had left the loft apartment for her visit with Kay, Nick still hadn't gotten home from work.

But a feral and haggard-looking Nick was pacing the floor when she got home. His hair hadn't seen a comb in quite some time, and he needed a shave. "Where've you been?"

"Excuse me?" she asked, slipping the strap of her purse off her shoulder and depositing the black bag onto the sofa.

He raked a hand through his hair, giving her a clue as to why it was mussed. "I'm sorry. I guess that was out of line."

"You told me I could use your car and that someone would bring you home. I didn't think—"

"It's not that," he said. "I was just worried, I guess. You know, that something happened to you."

No one had worried about Hailey in years. His concern was kind of nice, she supposed, touching, actually. "I went to see Kay."

"Good." His expression relaxed a tad. "How's everything going?"

"Fine." With Harry and Kay, anyway. "I've got something I'd like to talk to you about."

He plopped onto the sofa, stretched out his feet. "Have a seat."

She complied, but for some reason the words wouldn't form.

Today, more than ever, he bore a hard, rugged

edge. Maybe it was the result of working late last night, of the risks he'd taken because of his job.

For some reason she hated to mention anything now, not while he was sleep deprived and battle weary from a night on the city streets.

"Maybe you'd rather shower first," she said. "Or, better yet, get some rest?"

"I'm all right. Besides, I'm not sure I could fall asleep if I tried. Just tell me what's on your mind. Now's as good a time as any."

She wasn't so sure about that, but she doubted her revelation could wait much longer. Not now. Not when Kay already knew and had suggested that Harry would be pleased to welcome a new grandchild into the fold.

There was, she supposed, only one way to broach the subject. And that was head-on. "I'm going to have a baby."

His mouth dropped, and his eyes widened. "What?"

"A baby." She stood and walked to the window, searched the downtown streets for nothing in particular, other than a dose of courage. "In September sometime."

"September?"

She imagined him doing the math, calculating. Counting backward. And she turned, like an algebra teacher, waiting to see which child had come up with the right answer.

He wore an incredulous expression, as though his detective skills had failed him. "Is it mine?"

She had half a notion to throw an eraser at him, had she really been a math teacher and held one in her hand. "Of course it's yours."

"Oh, God," he said. She could have sworn he'd muttered the word in a frightened, desperate prayer rather than a lame effort at profanity.

"Don't worry, Nick. I won't ask anything of you. And in fact, if I didn't intend to return to California and be a part of Harry's life, I wouldn't have told you at all."

She wouldn't have told him?

Why the hell not? She couldn't keep something like that from him.

An argument, an objection jammed in his mouth, which he supposed was just as well. He was struck dumb. Nick Granger didn't take chances when it came to sex.

Except that one, snowy night in Minnesota.

The night Hailey had touched his heart and soul, made him forget right and wrong. Made him go all soft and mushy. Weak.

"I'm sorry," he said, as if that could fix everything and make things right.

"It's just as much my fault as yours," she said.

He supposed so, but he still felt irresponsible. Foolish. Left holding a bag he didn't know what to do with.

Hailey was pregnant. With his baby.

The very idea made him go all sappy inside, while at the same time it scared him senseless.

A baby?

A kid who would depend on Nick to point him or her in the right direction? To set an example?

"I don't expect anything from you," she added.

"What the hell is that supposed to mean?" He didn't mean to snap at her, it was just that this was all new to him. Her news had blindsided him. Made him feel inadequate.

She crossed her arms, facing him yet keeping her distance. "I'll raise the baby. As a single mother. You don't have to be a part of its life."

Not be a part of his kid's life?

Leave his son or daughter for someone else to raise, like his own father had done?

Let some other guy step in and take his place, someone who might be worse? Even more inadequate?

The thought made him want to puke—

The way she'd done on so many recent occasions. A nervous stomach, she'd said. But as far as he was concerned, she'd lied when she'd neglected to tell him it was morning sickness.

Was she ashamed of his part in all of this? Sorry that he'd participated in the conception?

So what if Nick had never planned on having kids. That didn't mean he wouldn't step up to the plate. *Somehow.*

Maybe if he were handed a kid about ten or twelve, he could manage. But an infant? A fragile little thing he'd probably drop and break? What did he know about babies? Or about parenting?

He glanced at her, caught her watching him with

a stoical expression. A guilty expression. Was she feeling badly about not telling him? Or was she just trying to decide whether he'd come to the same conclusion—that Nick wasn't father material. That he might screw up the kid's life.

For cripe's sake. She let him use a condom during lovemaking rather than tell him the truth. Why?

A myriad of emotions snowballed him. Anger that she hadn't wanted him to know about the baby. Fear that he wasn't the kind of guy who'd make a good father.

Hell, his own dad hadn't stuck around long enough to let Nick know what a real family was supposed to be like.

Hailey stood before him, looking strong yet vulnerable. Proud yet scared. In need of something he couldn't offer. An emotion he was afraid to admit, to give.

She needed someone special, a knight in shining armor. And Nick would fall short of the mark.

His mind drifted to the guy in Minnesota, the accountant. And a stab of jealousy pierced his soul. No, not that guy. Not some guy she already knew, someone she might choose over him.

Someone she might choose over him?

That kind of thinking was crazy. Nuts. Nick never had been the jealous kind. It couldn't be that. He was just tired. Hit from behind.

"I don't know what to say," he told her.

"You don't need to say anything." She brushed a

strand of hair from her eyes, big luminous eyes that bore an emotion he wasn't adept at reading.

Then she walked toward his closet and pulled out her canvas bag.

"Are you going home?" he asked, scared spitless that she was leaving for good.

He wanted to stop her, but he was too damn scared to beg her to stay, to tell her he needed her, that he wanted the baby—even though the whole family thing made him as nervous as a whore in church.

"I'm going to spend a few days with Kay and Harry," she said. "Until I have time to sort things out, to get some kind of game plan that I can live with."

Yeah, well he needed a game plan, too. He needed some time to figure out what in the hell he ought to do. What he ought to say.

His first inclination was to call his best friend and mentor, but he couldn't ask Harry for advice.

Not in this case.

Harry would probably shoot him point-blank. And Nick couldn't say that he'd blame him. Heck, his conscience would probably welcome the slug.

But just knowing the Logans would be there for Hailey, for the baby, was a big comfort. Yet the uneasiness remained, as well as the guilt.

He needed a shower. Some time to think.

Before he knew it, Hailey had packed her bag, then reached for the phone.

"Who are you calling?"

"A taxi."

"I'll take you wherever you need to go."

"I think it's best if we both have some time alone…if we take some time to think."

She might be right, but he wasn't letting her call a cab.

He took the phone from her hand. "Come on. I'll drive you to Kay's."

For a moment he thought she would argue, put up a fight. But she merely slipped the strap of her purse over her shoulder and grabbed her bag.

Twenty minutes later, in Bayside, Nick turned onto Harry's street. They'd ridden in silence, the news of Hailey's pregnancy hovering around them like a volatile gray rain cloud that threatened to burst.

Nick hadn't slept all night, leaving his senses dull, his emotions on edge. He needed time to clear his head. To figure out what he had to offer Hailey and the baby. Money was the easy part. He'd have no problem paying whatever was fair. More than was fair, he supposed. He didn't want his kid lacking anything.

His kid.

God, it was all so new. So surreal. So damn scary.

Nick stopped the Jeep in front of Harry's house.

"Don't bother walking me to the door," she said. "I'll be okay."

Would she? With Harry and Kay in her corner, she'd probably be just fine—one way or another.

But what about him?

For some reason his heart was thudding hard and

heavy in his chest, and he felt as though a rug had been jerked out from under his feet.

"I'll come back tomorrow," he said. "Then we can talk."

"It's not necessary."

"The hell it isn't." He raked his hand through his hair, then snagged her gaze in his. "Honey, give me some time to get used to this."

She nodded, then turned and strode up the walk to Harry's house.

Nick blew out a weary sigh. For some reason, he didn't think time would help him sort through much of anything. What did he know about babies? Or kids?

He watched Hailey fiddle with the key, open the door and step inside.

Maybe deep in her heart she understood. Maybe that's why she'd kept her secret from him until she had no other choice but to reveal it.

Hailey knew as well as he did that Nick Granger had nothing to offer a wife and kids.

Although he wished to God that he did.

Chapter Fourteen

Hailey spent the afternoon with Kay, sharing pieces of herself until she suspected the woman had put them all together like a patchwork quilt.

Or so it seemed.

They'd talked while sitting on the patio that afternoon and again while eating a light dinner of soup and tuna sandwiches. For the first time in years—maybe the first time ever—Hailey had a mother-daughter chat with a wise, kindhearted woman who cared about what she thought, what she felt, who she was.

Hailey had usually kept personal beliefs, feelings and dreams to herself, but Kay had an easy, gentle way about her, a maternal way that made intimacy seem natural.

Over the course of the day, she'd opened up and told Kay everything.

Well, not everything.

She'd kept the identity of her baby's father to herself.

But it hadn't been easy. She'd weakened several times, almost revealing her secret and baring her soul. And maybe she would have, had she truly understood what she actually felt for Nick, what would be in her heart if she allowed her feelings to rise to the surface.

"Do you love the baby's father?" Kay asked, as the women sat on the sofa in the cozy living room, wearing their nightclothes and sharing a cup of herbal tea before bed.

Hailey had never really asked herself that question, had never wanted to contemplate the answer. Maybe she'd begun to love Nick that first day she met him, that lonely night when they'd opened up to each other, shared the pain of their pasts. Reached out to each other and allowed that overwhelming rush of attraction to take over.

The night they'd made a baby.

She'd fought the growing attraction, tried to remain unaffected by the detective's rugged, bad-boy charm, his crooked smile, the depth of character she saw in those soulful brown eyes.

In spite of her best efforts, she'd grown to care for Nick. Deeply, and in a way that went much further than the sexual desire that weakened her knees and her resolve to stay on a steady keel.

She loved Nick Granger, a man who had the power to turn her life upside down.

A man who had done just that.

She released a sigh of surrender. "I do love him. More than I ever expected. But he doesn't love me."

Kay took a sip of tea, then held the cup with both hands instead of setting it down. "I assume you've told him how you feel about him."

Hailey slowly shook her head. "No, I've just admitted it to myself."

"Men are a tough breed," Kay said, a sympathetic smile gracing her face. "They're not always able to say what they feel. Perhaps you'll be surprised."

"Maybe so," she said, although she didn't plan to tell Nick she loved him. How could she lay open her heart to a man who didn't love her back?

He'd told her he wasn't husband and father material. And he certainly hadn't given her any reason to believe that he cared about her, not yesterday. Not when she could have used some loving words, a hug and a sympathetic ear. Not when she'd wanted him to say, "I love you, honey. And I want our baby. We're in this together."

"It took Harry ages to be able to say the words to me," Kay said. "But I knew he loved me. He showed it in a hundred different ways."

"It's not just hearing the words. I need to know that they ring true." Hailey looked to Kay for understanding, validation. "You don't think I sound like a hopeless romantic, do you?"

"Not at all." Kay reached out, took Hailey's hand and gave it a gentle squeeze. "You sound like a woman in love, a woman who needs to know that her man loves her, too. It's not too much to ask for."

"You know," Hailey said, "I've always wanted a family. And I feel as though you and my dad have offered me what I've been missing."

"I'm glad." Kay released her hand, but not the steady connection of her gaze. "But it's not enough, is it?"

"It would have been. Before I fell in love." Before she'd ridden the merry-go-round and had seen the prize held out for the taking. She offered Kay a wistful sigh. "But now I want it all."

She wanted the brass ring.

It might seem like such a small thing, minor in the scheme of things. But that solid brass circle, like a wedding ring, symbolized something that she would prize for the rest of her life. A promise. An unbroken bond that had no beginning, no end.

A love that wouldn't fail, a lover who wouldn't abandon her and the baby.

"Then I'll pray for you, Hailey. And I'll pray for that young man, too." Kay stood. "Come on, dear. Let's turn in for the night."

"Okay." But Hailey didn't think she'd be able to fall asleep for a long time.

Her heart was too empty.

And so were her outstretched hands, the hands that longed to hold that golden ring.

* * *

Nick had hoped a good night's sleep would clear his mind, help him sort through the news Hailey had given him.

But he'd slept like crap. And there was a wadded-up mound of sheets and blankets at this feet to prove it. Never had his bed felt so hard, so lumpy.

So damn empty.

When dawn crept over the city, bringing the light of day, he wasn't any more at ease with the whole baby situation.

But one thing had grown clear. Nick would do the right thing. He was going to ask Hailey to marry him and provide his child with a name and a home.

His child.

Would it be a boy or a girl? Would it look like Hailey, with her big blue eyes and pretty smile?

Or would the baby be a unique combination of them both?

It really didn't matter, he supposed. But it kind of tickled him to think of a little kid running around the house, a boy or a girl who was a part of him and Hailey. A child Hailey would be in charge of raising, because Nick damn sure wouldn't know the first thing about being a real dad—a guy who took an active part in his child's daily life. Nick would probably screw things up, fail the kid.

But on the other hand, Hailey would be a natural parent. And with Nick only too eager to take on the role of breadwinner, she wouldn't have to work, not while the baby was small. In fact, she wouldn't have to work at all, if she didn't want to.

Things might be a little tight financially, but he liked the idea of having her at home, making cookies, kissing boo-boos, being a mom.

And Hailey would be a great mother. She'd undoubtedly pick up the slack and compensate for his son or daughter having a dad who didn't know squat about kids.

A child would be lucky to have her.

A man, too.

Nick would actually look forward to coming home to Hailey's embrace, to the aroma of a meal baking in the oven or cooking on the stove. He could see himself unwinding in the evenings with Hailey—his wife. Imagine that. Nick and Hailey married.

A smile stole across his face as he envisioned them listening to music or cuddling in front of the television. He had to admit that even an occasional chick flick—watched together—wouldn't be so bad.

Then, when the night grew tired, he and Hailey would go to bed, where they would make love like there was no tomorrow. And when the time came for them to worry about birth control, they'd choose a convenient, married kind of contraceptive.

No more condoms, no more holding back, being careful—emotionally or otherwise.

Each morning for the rest of their lives he'd wake in Hailey's arms, feel that sense of comfort he'd had each time he'd slept with her.

Yep, being married to Hailey would definitely have an up side. For him, anyway, if not for her.

Nick knew he wasn't perfect—in a domestic sense. And he wasn't sure whether he wanted to be. There was only so much he was willing to change.

Sure, he and Hailey would probably fight like cats and dogs over the demands of his job, over the way he left the toilet lid up and ready for use. But even that kind of stuff didn't bother him as it had in the past. Not if he had Hailey to come home to, to turn his heart and soul every which way but loose.

They'd be great lovers. The best.

That had to count for something, didn't it? Sex was a biggie, as far as Nick was concerned. And he had every reason to suspect it would be important to Hailey, as well. Shouldn't that make her chalk one up for his side? Make her realize that Nick wasn't a complete failure in the dad and husband department?

By the time he'd showered and shaved, the whole concept of marrying Hailey and having a child together wasn't nearly as overwhelming as it had been the day before. In fact, he began to like the idea. A lot.

Now all he had to do was drive over to Kay and Harry's house. Talk to the mother of his child. Tell her he'd come up with a solution. Then he'd bring her back home, seal their promises by making love.

Yep. He had it all sorted out.

All he had to do was get her to agree to marry him.

How hard could that be? The plan made perfect sense to a realist like him.

Twenty minutes later Nick parked in front of the Logans' house, then began the walk toward the porch. A flood of anxiety swept over him. Apprehension, too. But he wasn't having any qualms about his decision to marry Hailey, about wanting to be a father to the baby. He was nervous about seeing her, facing her. Apologizing for not taking the news better yesterday. He actually was pretty happy about it now, all things considered.

He rang the bell, and moments later Kay answered the door. She gave him a hug in greeting, then welcomed him inside.

"I, uh, came by to see Hailey," he said, feeling like a goofy teenager with a corsage in his trembling hands.

"I'll tell her you're here."

Did Kay know? Had Hailey told her about the pregnancy? About who had fathered her baby?

If not, he supposed everyone would know soon enough.

Instead of feeling guilty, he actually experienced a strange surge of pride and a sappy warmth that swelled in his heart.

He was going to have a baby. And a pretty wife who could cross his eyes and curl his toes with a dimpled smile.

A family of his own.

Imagine that. Nick the loner would have someone to come home to, someone in his corner. And he'd be there for her and the baby, too.

When Hailey entered the room, he noted that her eyes looked red. Puffy.

Oh, man. The warm, swollen sense of pride burst, leaving him feeling like a coldhearted jerk. He didn't ever want to see Hailey cry again, didn't ever want to blame himself for her sadness.

He had the overwhelming urge to do something, say something. To quickly fix things, see her eyes brighten and make her smile again.

"Can I talk to you?" he asked. "Alone?"

She nodded, then asked Kay, "Would you excuse us?"

"Of course."

Hailey led Nick to the guest room. Once inside, he quickly scanned the pale-pink interior, the antique bed with a brass headboard, the white, fluffy comforter with frilly pillows. An overstuffed chaise upholstered in a pink floral print sat in the corner by a window adorned with white ruffled curtains.

Had Hailey slept here last night? Was this the room Kay had given her? He thought so. The girly decor suited her.

Would Hailey decorate his place like this, adding a feminine touch and leaving her gentle mark?

It wouldn't bother him if she did. His home was lacking something, although he'd never noticed before.

"Have a seat," she said, like a prim and proper hostess.

Nick hated to sit on the spread, thinking he'd probably get it dirty or mess it up, so he chose the corner of the chaise.

Hailey sat on the edge of the mattress, braced for

a confrontation. But she wouldn't get a fight from him. He was already thinking about the kiss and hug part of all of this. The part when he would tell Kay they were going back home, to his place.

"I kind of botched up our conversation yesterday," he said.

"You were tired. And I'm sure it came as quite a shock."

She had that right. But that didn't change things. Hailey was expecting his baby. A child who hadn't asked to be born, who hadn't been given a list of fathers to choose from.

"I've had some time to think things through," he told her.

"And?" Hailey asked, her hands folded in her lap.

"And I want to marry you." There, he'd said it. And it still felt good. Right.

Her brow furrowed. "You what?"

Hadn't she heard him? Or was she questioning the wisdom of a move like that?

"For the baby's sake," he explained. "Ours, too." Then, in case she needed the reminder, he added, "We're sexually compatible, to say the least."

She stood and crossed her arms, not at all looking as though she appreciated him offering to do the right thing. Or appreciating the reference to their sexual relationship, although he wasn't sure why.

"There's more to marriage than sex."

"I know," he said, although he didn't think a marriage without sex—or with lousy sex—was anything to shout about. Yet he wasn't sure what more she'd want out of a relationship, what more he could give. "We get along well. And I've got a stable job, health benefits, a pension."

"I think marriages should be based on love."

Maybe she was right, but he wasn't sure what love was, wasn't sure that he was lovable or that he could love anyone. And he sure as heck couldn't imagine romance and mushy words in his future. Nick Granger wasn't a hearts-and-flowers kind of guy.

He knew this situation would take some work, some careful maneuvering on his part.

"We need to think of the baby," he said. "I want to give him or her my name. I want to do the right thing, Hailey."

The right thing?

Hailey wanted to do the right thing, too. But could she marry the father of her baby, just to make things "right"?

She wanted so much more out of marriage than a name for her baby. She wanted more from the man she'd grown to love in spite of herself.

Her feelings for Nick had surprised her, since he was so out of sync with her image of a dream mate. But she did love him. Deeply.

She supposed her love might be enough for both of them, but love was a two-way street, the bond that held a marriage and family together. The best guarantee she had for a commitment that would last a lifetime. It was the one part of the dream she couldn't give up, that she wouldn't compromise.

"I can't marry a man who doesn't love me."

Nick furrowed his brow, struggling, it seemed, with his emotions. Or maybe just with the truth.

"What does love have to do with it?" He looked at her, searching for an answer that should be clear to him.

"Love helps a couple weather the storms." It seemed a bit trite, she supposed, so she dug deeper. "It's what makes life special."

"Things have been pretty special so far." He smiled, and she suspected he was talking about the sex. Or maybe he'd picked up on how nice it was to be together, holding hands and window-shopping along the beach walk in Bayside. Listening to the romantic ballad of mariachis in Old Town. Riding on the carousel with her in Balboa Park. "Isn't that enough?"

It was close. Very close. But it wasn't enough. And it was time they both faced the reason why it wasn't. As much as she feared his rejection, his abandonment, she forced herself to be honest. "I didn't mean for it to happen, Nick. But I fell in love with you."

A look of panic washed over his face, yet he didn't respond, he just watched her with the eyes of a cornered animal. A wild critter who wanted to bolt.

She might have sympathized with him if her heart wasn't splitting at the seams. "I can't marry a man who doesn't love me back."

Nick ran his hand through his hair, then caught her gaze and blew out a sigh. "I'm sorry, Hailey. I don't know how to love you back."

The truth of his words was etched deeply on his face, and she let reality settle around them.

"I'll try my best to make you happy. To be a good provider. But what you're asking...I don't know what love is. I can't say..."

She nodded, appreciating the fact that he wouldn't lie, wouldn't utter an I-love-you as an attempt to sway her and not really mean it in a till-death-do-us-part sense. "Thanks for your honesty."

"I know marriage is something you've always wanted. I remember the *Modern Brides* magazine you had on your coffee table."

She had wanted marriage. And she still did. But she wanted it all—white lace, promises, a gold band. An unending circle of love that would last a lifetime.

"I wish you'd reconsider marrying me." His expression was that of a lost and forlorn little boy.

The fact that he could display his feelings, although not the emotion she'd been hoping for, touched her heart. His decency and insistence on doing the right thing drew her admiration. But it wasn't enough to sell out, to give up what she so desperately wanted. What she needed. What she deserved.

"No, Nick. I can't marry you. But you can be a part of the baby's life, if you'd like to."

He nodded but didn't speak. He merely pressed his lips together as though holding back the words, keeping his thoughts and deeper feelings to himself.

They sat there for a while, as though each of them was waiting for the other to bend, to accept less.

"I'm not going to beg. It's not my style," he said,

standing and shoving his hands in his pockets. "I guess I'd better go."

She nodded but didn't respond. She didn't trust her voice not to choke out a sob, not to agree to a marriage based on great sex.

"Mind if I use your bathroom?" he asked, his eyes looking misty. Or maybe she'd just looked at him through her own watery gaze.

"Go ahead." She sat back on the bed, waited, hoping the time alone would allow her to swallow her disappointment and blink back the tears that gathered in her eyes.

The water in the sink ran, but the toilet didn't flush. And when he walked out the door, his face appeared damp, as though he might have tried to wash away the signs of his disappointment, his sadness.

Aw, heck. There she went, reading into things again. Imagining that Nick had to wash his own tears away.

A tough guy like Nick Granger didn't get weepy or cry.

And he wouldn't admit to loving someone unless it was true.

"I'd like to start paying some child support before the baby is born," he said, his gravelly voice a little softer than usual. "You'll probably need to get a lot of things."

His consideration touched her broken heart, applying a balm. "Thanks. But we can talk about that later."

"Yeah."

Then he strode out of the room, softly closing the door and leaving her to break down and cry alone.

And she did cry—for the longest time, even though she'd bawled her eyes out last night and thought she couldn't possibly have any tears left.

When the sobbing subsided, leaving her with an ache she feared would never go away, she went into the bathroom to wash her face, to cool her eyes. To freshen up and try to hide her pain.

Her gaze drifted to the towel rack, where she expected to see the towels uneven, messed up and in need of straightening.

But Nick had left them just as neatly as he'd found them.

Hailey took the towel he'd used to dry his hands, his face, and tugged until it hung unevenly, the way it belonged, the way he'd left her heart and her life—skewed.

At least in some small way he was still with her—messy, unstructured. Unpredictable.

She stared at the towels until the image blurred, twisted. Until nothing remained clear except the ache in her heart.

Chapter Fifteen

Nick paced the floor of the loft apartment he'd once called home, feeling like a caged animal—one that had been seriously wounded and didn't know which way to turn, which way to strike.

He hadn't seen Hailey in days, hadn't even talked to her, since he wasn't sure what to say, wasn't sure how to convince her to marry him.

The longer they spent apart, the more Nick wanted to bring her home. To his place. But short of hog-tying her and throwing her over his shoulder like a Neanderthal, which certainly wouldn't be the romantic approach a woman like her would appreciate, he couldn't think of any other way.

More than ever, Nick missed having Harry in his

corner, the one friend who had always offered him good, solid advice when he asked for it.

Well, he was on his own this time.

Alone.

For a guy who'd always been a loner, who'd always enjoyed playing by his own rules, the wave of loneliness that slammed into him this time made it hard to breathe.

He had to shake it off, had to figure out what to do, how to convince Hailey that marrying a guy like him was worth the risk. That they could make it— together.

Nick and Hailey.

And their baby.

There'd be three of them, making a small family. He envisioned an image of Hailey nursing his baby, then rocking the infant to sleep. Tying his toddler's shoes. But each time he caught a glimpse of mother and child, he felt like a portrait on the wall, a still, silent voyeur who was unable to join in.

Okay. So he really *did* want to be a part of his kid's life, a part of its mother's life. But did he dare admit it to Hailey? Admit his fear of inadequacy? Agree to give it his best shot, anyway?

Did he dare lay his heart on the line? Tell Hailey that he really cared for her? *A lot?*

That he might even love her? The way she deserved to be loved?

Hell, Nick couldn't ever remember loving anyone, or being loved in return. He wouldn't even recognize the emotion if it sneaked up and kissed him on the lips.

Like Hailey had done to him, pressing her heart against his chest, placing her arms around his neck, lifting her lips to his. Putting some kind of hold on him that he couldn't shake, couldn't break.

Was that love?

Some sappy bond you couldn't see, couldn't explain, yet couldn't imagine giving up or living without?

If so, love had sneaked up on him. And like a fool, he'd let it slip away. He'd let Hailey go without a fight. But how did one go about fighting an invisible foe? Confronting something he couldn't see, couldn't touch?

The phone rang, more than once, and it took him a moment to actually hear it. He snatched the receiver and answered, "Granger."

"Hello, Nick. It's Kay."

Was something wrong? With Hailey or the baby? Nick's heart thudded in his chest. A surge of worry, fear and something else shot through his blood. "What's the matter?"

"Nothing, dear. I just wanted to invite you to dinner. Harry's home now. And we thought it might be nice to have company this evening."

We thought it might be nice? Did *we* mean Kay and Harry? Or had Hailey taken part in the invitation?

"I'm not sure how Hailey will feel about me coming over," Nick said, hoping to pry some additional information from Kay. Some word of how Hailey was doing. A hint of what she might be thinking. About him. Them.

"She's doing fine," Kay said. "Of course, I think she's spending too much time in her room. I thought having company might give her something to look forward to."

Hailey had been locked up in her room? Was she sick? Or just mad at him for not being more sensitive to her needs and able to say the things she wanted to hear? It was hard to tell. Could she possibly be missing him? Wishing she'd given the idea of their marriage more thought?

Maybe things had changed. Maybe she would be happy to see him. God, he hoped so. He was missing her something fierce.

"Hailey wasn't too pleased with me the other day," he admitted to Kay.

"She's going through a lot right now."

Nick knew that. Hell, he was going through a lot, too. A lot of emotional stuff he wasn't used to.

But he needed to take responsibility for his part of the situation. And there was no use skirting the truth.

"I'm to blame for most of her problems," he said, unable to actually come right out and say, I'm the bastard who got your daughter pregnant. The hard-ass who probably loves her but can't come clean and admit it. The tough guy who's afraid to face the consequences of a revelation like that.

"I see," Kay said, although Nick wasn't sure what

she "saw." He was still trying to clear his mind, make sense of the obscurity.

"I want to make things right, but I don't know how."

The older woman didn't respond immediately, as though she was still putting clues together. Or maybe she was just trying to decide how to tell Nick he was a jerk. And that Hailey would be a fool to marry a guy like him.

"A woman's feelings are pretty tender at a time like this."

Yeah, well, for a guy with a cast-iron heart, his feelings were pretty damn tender, too. Raw. Painful. And way too close to the surface.

"I guess that's to be expected," Nick said, although he didn't understand much of anything about what Hailey was going through, about what either one of them could expect next.

"Don't worry, Nick. She'll be all right. With time."

But Nick didn't want her to be all right, not if it meant she was going to pull together without him, without even looking back.

For some reason, he wanted Kay to know how he felt about Hailey. "I care about her. *A lot.*"

"I can understand that. She's a lovely young woman."

They were, it seemed, still skating around the issue, around the reality. Hailey was pregnant with Nick's baby. And even though he'd offered marriage, she'd refused to accept. And that hurt, way more than he'd expected.

With each tick of the old-style, windup clock on the nightstand, he grew more aware of how lonely and miserable his life would be without Hailey in it, without her pretty smile, the lilt of her laugh.

"This is tough on me, Kay. I'm not a sensitive guy. And Hailey needs so much more than I can give."

Again she paused. "Sometimes it's hard to put feelings into words."

"You've got that right." He plowed a hand through his hair, scanned the vast emptiness of an apartment that had always seemed just fine—before Hailey had blessed it with her touch, her scent, her presence.

"So," Kay said. "Can we set another plate on the table this evening?"

"Yeah," Nick said, trying to gather his thoughts together. "Sure, I'd like that, Kay."

When he hung up the phone, things started to fall into place—at least better than they had before.

He had a reason to go to Harry's house, a reason to bust in on Hailey and see her one more time. Talk to her. Get her to see reason. Tell her the one thing that might convince her that taking a chance and making a home with Nick wouldn't be so bad.

And if it didn't help?

Then what did he have left to lose?

He already felt broken and empty.

* * *

When Nick arrived at the Logans', Kay met him at the door before he got a chance to ring the bell.

"Harry's upstairs resting. I'll let him know you're here."

"Thanks."

"In the meantime," she said, "Hailey's in the kitchen. You might stop in there and tell her hello."

Nick actually felt a stab of nervousness. A flutter in his pulse.

Was it a setup? A carefully orchestrated plan to get him and Hailey together? Women did things like that sometimes, tried to fix things. Used a strategy known only to them.

Had Kay tried to help a crippled relationship mend?

Nick sure hoped so. He was going to need all the help he could get.

When he reached the kitchen, he spotted Hailey before she saw him. She wore a pink T-shirt and a pair of faded jeans. Nothing fancy, yet he found himself gawking.

She stood at the counter, holding an electric mixer while mashing potatoes, her mind on her work, her brow furrowed in concentration. She didn't wear any makeup to speak of, other than a light glossy sheen to her lips. But she didn't need any props.

Pretty Hailey could touch his heart with a smile. She glanced out the kitchen window, a wistful look on her face.

His heart did a double flip, landing in a belly flop, and he just stared at her like a moonstruck kid.

What he wouldn't give to come home every night and find her in his kitchen. Or curled up on the sofa, reading a book. Or playing with their baby on the floor.

He longed to take her in his arms, tell her he was home, see her face light up. Kiss her with all the passion he'd bottled up during the day.

Instead he just said, "Hi."

She turned, her eyes growing wide, her lips parting.

Okay, so Kay hadn't told her he'd been invited for dinner, but since she'd answered the door before the bell could alert Hailey to his presence, he figured she'd been playing matchmaker. That she'd tried to force Hailey and Nick into being together, talking. Maybe she hoped they could work things out.

But that was the extent of Kay's orchestrating.

Nick was on his own now.

Hailey flipped the switch on the mixer, silencing the sound of the small motor.

"Kay invited me to dinner," he said.

"Oh." Her face seemed to fall.

Disappointed? Hoping that he'd come on his own with something to say?

"I want to apologize," he said.

"For what?" She leaned her hip against the kitchen drawers that supported the countertop. "Being honest? I can't fault you for that."

"I wasn't being honest."

She lifted a brow, watched him. Tried to read him.

Well, good luck. He was still trying to figure himself out.

"I've spent years trying to convince myself that I didn't need anyone, not a woman, not a family." He sought her gaze, her understanding. Her compassion, too, he supposed. "It was the only way I could survive in a world where no one gave a damn about me."

He kind of hoped she'd step in and tell him that she cared about him, remind him that she loved him. But she merely stood there, arms crossed as though guarding her heart.

"This is all new to me," he said.

She placed a hand on the still-flat plane of her tummy, the spot where his baby grew. "It's new to me, too."

"I wasn't talking about the baby." He wanted to step closer, to take her in his arms when he told her. To say the words while she looked the other way. But that would be cheating.

"What's new to you?" she asked, her voice soft, laden with emotions he'd yet to decipher.

Just days ago she'd said that she loved him. Wasn't it the lasting kind of love? The kind that might overlook the way Nick was sure to screw up this conversation?

"This is new. The rush of feelings I get whenever I think of you. Me. Us."

If she understood what he meant, she wasn't making it easy for him.

"I've never been in love before," he admitted, hoping she'd cut him some slack.

Her brow lifted. Her head tilted slightly. "And?"

He took a deep breath, then slowly let it go. "No one has ever loved me before, either."

She merely stood there, leaning against the kitchen counter, waiting, it seemed, for him to lay open his stubborn heart.

"I've been running from love ever since I was a kid, ever since I realized that home wasn't somewhere I wanted to be. And when it came time to move out and get a place of my own, I was just glad to come home to four walls and some peace and quiet. No yelling. No bitching. No drunken brawls and accusations."

Her lip twitched and her eyes glistened. She was listening. And feeling something.

He wasn't wanting her sympathy, though. Just her understanding.

"I feel something for you, Hailey. Something powerful. Something warm. And I tried hard to ignore it." He raked a hand through his hair, then crossed his arms. "I didn't realize being in love felt like this."

"Felt like what?"

She was making him go the distance, spit it out. Lay it all on the table. Well, if that's the way she wanted it, then he'd spill his guts. And his heart.

"That being in love would make me feel so crazy about you. It's this powerful I-gotta-have-Hailey-with-me feeling that dogs me wherever I go."

Was that enough? Was she getting it? Would she help him through the romantic muck and mire and cut to the chase?

It didn't appear likely, so he continued to stumble and fumble on his own. "I love you, Hailey."

Her arms dropped, her lips parted. Her eyes brightened. "You do? Are you sure?"

That was all the push he needed. He crossed the kitchen in two steps, took her in his arms and held her tight, losing himself in her apricot scent, in her soft embrace.

He pressed a kiss against her hair. "Yeah, I'm sure, Hailey. But the bad part is knowing that I'm not the kind of guy a woman like you needs."

She didn't argue, didn't put up a fight. But she held him tightly, as though she might never let go.

That had to count for something, didn't it?

"Are you in this for the duration?" she asked. "I don't want my baby to grow up without a dad, to feel abandoned if you change your mind."

"I'm not going anywhere, honey. Not now that I've got you in my life and figured out what love is. Not when I want to make a family with you." Nick pulled away, just far enough to see her eyes, to cup her face. "I'm not a romantic guy, Hailey. And God knows I'm far from perfect. I don't ride a white horse, and I can't carry you off into the sunset. But I love you. And I swear on all that's holy to give everything I've got to our marriage, our relationship. To you and the baby."

Nick loved her.

Hailey couldn't ask for any more than that. Tears welled in her eyes as she saw the love glowing in his eyes.

"What do you say?" he asked. "Will you marry me?"

"Are we talking weddings?"

He scrunched his face. "I should have known a simple little service in front of a justice of the peace wouldn't be good enough for a woman who reads bride magazines."

"It would just be a small wedding."

"How small? You, me and a preacher?"

"Bigger than that."

"Will I have to wear a tux?"

"And a smile," she said. "You'd have to be happy about it."

Nick kissed her, then slid her that crooked grin she'd never grow tired of looking at. "I'm happier than I've ever been."

"Me, too," she said. Then she slipped her arms around his neck, pulled him back into her embrace. "I love you, Nick Granger. With all my heart."

Then they sealed their love with a kiss.

In a small room off to the side of the Park Avenue Community Church, Nick fiddled with the bow tie on his tuxedo.

"Can you believe I'm wearing one of these monkey suits in broad daylight, before God and practically the whole city of San Diego?" Nick asked Harry.

His old friend and soon-to-be-father-in-law laughed. "You'll do just fine. I always knew some woman would soften your edges. I just didn't realize that woman would be my little girl."

"Yeah, well, she's left her mark on me."

"Is that so bad?" Harry asked.

"Nope. I've got to admit, I like the changes she's made in me, in my life."

Harry placed a hand on Nick's shoulder. "You know, I've always thought of you as a son. Now I guess it's official."

"This family stuff is kind of new to me, Harry, but I'm looking forward to being a husband and a father. A son, too."

Harry wrapped him in a bear hug. "Just treat my little girl right."

"I will. But speaking of your little girl, I was hoping she'd agree to a simple, outdoor wedding. You know, something on the shore in La Jolla, or maybe even in Bayside. Something laid-back and easy, where the bridal party and guests didn't wear shoes."

"Once Kay and Hailey put their heads together, you and I didn't have anything to say about this. All we had to do was put on a tux and show up."

A light rap sounded at the door, then Joe Davenport, Nick's friend and best man, entered the room.

"It's time," Joe said.

Yep, it was time, Nick thought. Time to marry the woman he loved. Time to give their baby a name and a home. Time to create the kind of family that he and Hailey had never known. The kind of family she'd always dreamed of.

Him, too, if truth be told, but he'd never allowed that dream to surface. Not until Hailey entered his life and turned his lonely world on end.

Moments later Nick stood at the quaint old church that Kay and Harry had attended for years. Fellow bad boy and fireman Joe Davenport stood at his side as Nick waited for Hailey to walk down the aisle.

Music from an old pipe organ began, and Maria, Hailey's sister-in-law, started down the aisle. Moments later, the organist began the first chords of the bridal march, and Harry escorted pretty Hailey down a flower-petal-strewn, white-carpeted walkway. Her smile, so happy and full of love, took Nick's breath away and shot hope and promises through his core.

When his bride neared the altar, a heartbeat away from Nick's arms, Reverend Morton asked, "Who gives this woman away?"

Harry cleared his throat and said in a loud, booming voice, "Her mother and I."

In short order, the scripture was read, prayers were spoken and the vows were made. Then Nick kissed his wife with all the love in his heart.

But the wedding wasn't over yet.

"Please join Mr. And Mrs. Granger as they begin their lives together," Reverend Morton said. Then he nodded, and Nick took Hailey by the hand.

As they reached the front steps of the church, a line of horse-drawn carriages awaited them.

"What's going on?" Hailey asked, clearly aware

of the fact they hadn't rehearsed this part, that climbing in a carriage wasn't in her carefully laid wedding plans. "Where are we going?"

"For a ride through Balboa Park."

Hailey glanced behind her, saw Harry and Kay climbing into one of the carriages, too, along with the others.

"This is sweet," Hailey said. "And romantic."

Nick took her hand in his. "I guess you bring out all kinds of crazy things in me."

Hailey blessed him with a smile. "I'm glad."

As they rode through the park, the dappled sunlight danced through the trees. And ten minutes later they drew near the carousel.

"Oh, look," Hailey said, her voice soft and wistful.

When the carriage pulled to a stop in front of the merry-go-round and Nick climbed out, she asked, "What are you doing?"

Nick slid her a crooked grin and reached out to her. "You have to snag the brass ring, honey. It won't fall in your hands."

The carousel slowed to a stop, and Nick ushered Hailey aboard, lifted her onto the pony she favored. And as the crowd of brand-new family and old friends clapped, the merry-go-round started up.

Military-band-style music played, and the carousel ponies and zoo animals began to circle. Hailey, looking prettier than any bride magazine cover girl, broke into a laugh. "And you told me you weren't a romantic guy."

"Having a wife brings out the best in me." He kissed her softly on the lips, then nodded up ahead. "There it is."

"What if we miss?" she asked. "There are a lot of kids riding this thing."

"I've got a wad of cash in my pocket. I'll keep buying us tickets until we win."

The man who ran the carousel extended the wooden arm that held the rings, some of them iron, only one of them brass.

A child riding a tiger grabbed for the displayed ring—one made of dull gray—leaving a shiny, golden circle for Nick and Hailey.

Together they reached for the brass ring, the prize they'd both been hoping for.

Love that would bind them forever.

And when they held it in their hands, Nick turned to her and smiled, his eyes glimmering with love.

"Happy now?" he asked.

"Happier than any bride has a right to be." Then she wrapped her arms around his neck, kissing him with all the love in her heart.

"I know what you mean," he said. "I'm going to like having you as my wife."

"And as your lover?"

"I never made any secrets about that." He winked, then flashed her that crooked smile she'd grown to adore. "Let's get the reception underway so we can cut out early. I'm looking forward to starting the happily-ever-after stuff."

"Me, too," Hailey told him.

But it had already started, the happiness, the dream come true, the promise of forever.

It had begun the day she met Nick—her friend, her lover, her hero.

Turn the page for a sneak preview of
THEIR SECRET SON
Silhouette Special Edition #1667,
the next book in
Judy Duarte's miniseries
BAYSIDE BACHELORS.
Available February 2005!

Chapter One

With every call to a fire, a shot of pure adrenaline coursed through Joe Davenport's blood and didn't let up until the last hot spot was out. And this one was no different.

The scent of ash filled the air as Joe walked through the charred weeds that once blanketed the vacant lot on the corner of Tidal Way and Harbor View Drive, searching for a point of origin. He spotted it near a melted blob of blackened plastic.

Rookie fireman, Dustin Campbell, strode toward Joe, his hand clamped on the shoulder of a kid who looked no more than seven years old. "We've got us a firebug, Joe. I caught him standing in the copse of trees, and he smells like smoke."

The boy wore a crisp pair of khaki slacks with dirt

and grass stains on the knees. A suspicious bulge rested in the ash-smudged pocket of a freshly pressed, white button-down shirt.

"What do you have there, son?"

The towheaded boy, whose clothing suggested he'd grown up in a well-to-do home, shrugged, then reached into his pocket, withdrew a gold, monogrammed cigarette lighter and handed it over without any qualms.

Joe had no intention of scaring the kid, but a serious talk about the dangers of playing with matches or lighters, followed by an offer to make the youngster a junior fire marshal usually worked like a charm.

He assessed the boy with a narrowed eye of authority. "What's your name?"

"Bobby." The boy stood as tall as a seven-year-old stance would allow. The small, squared chin told Joe he'd have to practice his intimidation skills a bit more.

With a cowlick that refused to obey a comb or gel, a scatter of freckles across his nose and a dirt-smudged cheek, the boy reminded Joe a lot of himself at that age.

Joe had also been a cocky, towheaded kid, prone to trouble. But he shook off the comparison. "Did you start the fire?"

"Nope." Bobby crossed his arms and shifted his weight to one side.

"But you must have seen it."

Bobby shrugged his small shoulders in a cocky defense that reminded Joe of his own run-in with the law after starting a fire in an abandoned building when he was a kid. Joe hadn't meant to do anything other than draw attention to his father's illegal activities.

His old man had been dealing crack from that building for years, and Joe decided to do something about it, something that would make the firefighters and cops take notice. As a fourteen-year-old, he'd hoped the efforts of men in authority might cause a drug-addicted dad to see reason.

That day, nearly twelve years ago, had been a real turning point in his life.

Once charged with arson and delinquency, Joe Davenport was now well on his way to becoming a fire chief, thanks to the guidance of Harry Logan, patron saint of bad boys.

"How do you suppose the fire started?" Joe asked Bobby.

"It was my mom's fault," the kid said.

Now the story was getting interesting. Joe remained focused and controlled, but a grin tugged at his lips. "Suppose you tell me why it was her fault."

The boy took a deep breath, then blew out a sigh, as though frustrated he had to explain something that should have been apparent. "I got a model car for my birthday, and some of the little prongs that hold the parts together broke off. I asked her if I could use her nail glue, cause it works good enough to stick your fingers together forever, but she wouldn't let me.''

Joe raised a brow, but refrained from showing any other expression. ''So she started the field on fire?''

''No. I had to figure out another way to make it stick together. Then I remembered how plastic melts, cause once I stuck a plastic fork in the fireplace and it melted into a glob that got real hard. So I took my grandpa's lighter, even though I'm not s'posed to play with it, but I was gonna be real careful.'' The boy's hazel eyes shimmered, and his bottom lip quivered in what looked like his first bit of remorse. ''And the car caught the field on fire when it melted.''

At the boy's defensive explanation, Joe considered turning his back so the kid wouldn't see him grin at a child's logic. How did parents deal with this stuff on a daily basis? This boy needed some firm, loving guidance.

Not a fist, of course, which had been his own father's way of dealing with a strong-willed child. Joe wasn't an expert on child rearing by any means, but he knew what didn't work.

''Bobby!'' a woman's voice called from across the street.

So, the mother had arrived. Well, Joe had a little talk for mothers of small-fry firebugs, too. Gearing himself for a confrontation, he slowly turned around.

But nothing had prepared him for seeing Kristin Reynolds, a woman he'd dated eight years ago. She was still just as pretty as he remembered, tall and willowy, with hair the color of honey and eyes emerald green.

The years had been good to her. *Damn good.*

His heart slipped into overdrive, reminding him his blood was pumping in all the important places. There were some things time didn't change.

The pretty socialite hurried toward them, with an expression that looked a lot like maternal concern.

Surely Kristin wasn't this kid's mother.

Her scent, something classy and exotic—expensive, no doubt—wrapped around him like a quilt of memories on a cold and lonely night.

Joe cursed under his breath. How could she still evoke this kind of reaction in him—both emotionally and physically?

It had been eight years since he'd last held her. And it had taken ages to get over her.

"I'm okay, Mom," the boy said.

Joe looked at Bobby, and suddenly the similarities he'd seen in the kid slapped him across the face. His mind, although somewhat unbalanced and taken aback, did a quick calculation, starting with eight years and subtracting nine months.

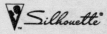

SPECIAL EDITION™

This month, Silhouette Special Edition
brings you the newest
Montana Mavericks story

ALL HE EVER WANTED
(SE #1664)

by reader favorite

Allison Leigh

When young Erik Stevenson fell down an abandoned
mine shaft, he was lucky to be saved by a brave—and
beautiful—rescue worker, Faith Taylor. She was struck by
the feelings that Erik's handsome father, Cameron, awoke
in her scarred heart and soul. But Cameron's heart had
barely recovered from the shock of losing his wife some
time ago. Would he be able to put the past aside—and
find happiness with Faith in his future?

GOLD RUSH GROOMS

Lucky in love—and striking it rich—
beneath the big skies of Montana!

**Don't miss this emotional story—
only from Silhouette Books.**

Available at your favorite retail outlet.

Where love comes alive™

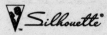

SPECIAL EDITION™

presents:

Bestselling author

Susan Mallery's

next installment of

Watch how passions flare under the hot desert sun for these rogue sheiks!

THE SHEIK & THE BRIDE WHO SAID NO

(#1666, available February 2005)

Daphne Snowden called off her wedding to Crown Prince Murat ten years ago and now he wanted her back. The passionate flames of their past were reigniting, and Murat *always* got what he wanted. But now the woman he loved was saying "no" when all he wanted to hear was "yes"....

Available at your favorite retail outlet.

Where love comes alive™

If you enjoyed what you just read,
then we've got an offer you can't resist!

Take 2 bestselling love stories FREE!

Plus get a FREE surprise gift!

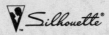

SPECIAL EDITION™

Discover why readers love
Judy Duarte!

From bad boys to heroes…
through the love of a good woman.

The tow-headed son of stunning socialite Kristin Reynolds
had to be his. Because, once upon a time, fireman
Joe Davenport and Kristin had been lovers, but were
pulled apart by her family. Now, they were both adults.
Surely Joe could handle parenthood without reigniting
his old flame for the woman who tempted him to want
the family—and the wife—he could never have.

THEIR SECRET SON
by Judy Duarte
Silhouette Special Edition #1667
On sale February 2005

Meet more Bayside Bachelors later this year!
WORTH FIGHTING FOR—Available May 2005
THE MATCHMAKER'S DADDY—Available June 2005

Only from Silhouette Books!

Where love comes alive™